How You Can Make $30,000 a Year as a Musician

How You Can Make $30,000 a Year as a Musician Without a Record Contract

James Gibson

Writer's Digest Books

Cincinnati, Ohio

Library of Congress Cataloging in Publication Data

Gibson, James R., 1944-
  How you can make $30,000 a year as a musician—without a record contract.
  Bibliography: p.
  Includes index.
    1. Music—Economic aspects. 2. Music—Vocational guidance. 3. Music trade—United
States. I. Title. II. Title: How you can make thirty thousand dollars a year as a musician—
without a record contract.
ML3795.G52   1986   780'.23'73   85-31533
ISBN 0-89879-214-2

Design by Joan Ann Jacobus

*To Sandra, Chris, Laura
and my parents . . . music
lovers all*

Contents

1
Are You Good Enough?   5

Know when you're ready by visiting jobs you'd like to be playing. Notice styles, ask questions, learn the repertoire, polish your showmanship. Use home audiovisual equipment to fine-tune your performance skills. Learn from the pros, maybe as an apprentice. Know what the job really is, and make sure you measure up.

2
Why You Need a Job-Finding System   11

You can make a steady, high-paying career out of one-night stands it the stands are in good places and the nights are close enough together. You need to know the conditions in your musical field and decide whether you'd do better to organize a new group or join one that's already established. Maybe you should do both, *and* become a musical contractor, *and* solo on the side. For that, you'll need a job-finding system.

3
The Basic Idea: Music Is a Product   17

Start out facing the facts of the marketplace. Clients expect to get what they pay for, not just what you happen to like. But every profession has its tradeoffs, and doing what *they* like can support you in doing what *you* like. Besides musical satisfactions, you'll learn the satisfaction of "a professional job well done." The bottom line is always finding enough people who like your music enough to pay for it.

4
Music Is a Business   21

A successful musician is part salesperson, advertising specialist, secretary, accountant, stage manager, sound engineer, equipment mover, and much more. You need to build up contacts and learn to "network"—in person, by phone, and by mail—not wait for the jobs to come beating on your door. Learn to do the paperwork that will keep your career rolling along, and present a professional appearance in all your operations.

5
Developing Your Personal Music-Marketing System   29

Keep out of the ruts that can kill your love of music, but stay interested (and financially stable) by scheduling a variety of jobs that will help keep your enjoyment and your musicianship fresh.

6
Your Personal Inventory   35

Evaluate your musical strengths, the equipment and instruments you can use, and your abilities—personal and professional—so you really know what you have to offer. Use this information in seeking and scheduling dates. Plan for success.

7
Your Job Possibilities List   47

Locate as many possible kinds of jobs as you can—jobs that will need, could use, or might possibly benefit from your music. The more potential job categories you include, the more you'll work and the more money you'll make. Job possibilities come from experience, imagination, creative brainstorming, and a little market research. There are more opportunities, in more likely and unlikely places, than you'd guess until you really start thinking and listing.

8
Kinds of Jobs That Need You   51

If you're considering nightclubs (and you should), know what kind of a club each is and what the management expects. Be ready for the physical and mental demands, and get a written contract. Be ready for occasional work as well as longer engagements. Restaurants, hotels, colleges and schools, weddings, bar mitzvahs, country clubs, and parties in homes are also good markets for live music. And if you spread your name around, you may be hired as a pinch-drummer or vocalist, leading to still more contacts in your growing network.

9
More Jobs   65
Industry likes music too. Public relations firms and advertising agencies can be good music clients; conventions are booming and shopping malls are sprouting everywhere, providing a rapidly expanding market for freelance musicians. Then there are sales meetings, ground-breaking ceremonies, fashion shows, grand openings, and trade shows, as well as the more personal business events: promotions, retirements, and Christmas parties. Civic, social, governmental, and nonprofit organizations often hold celebrations and festivals and are additional consumers of live music that you should consider.

10
Still More Jobs   79
Amateur and professional theaters need music and offer an excellent way to get experience and meet people in your field. Circuses, traveling shows, sports events, tourist attractions, and theme parks often have music as one of their regular features. Orchestras, dance bands, churches and synagogues, radio and TV stations, and recording studios also provide opportunities. You might teach, work in music therapy, work as a music librarian, or write as a music critic for a magazine or newspaper. You could add instrument repair or sales, making musical arrangements, or booking musical acts to your repertoire of skills. Or had you thought about delivering a singing telegram, writing jingles, or becoming a street musician?

11
Your Best Possibilities   97
With a long list of possible jobs, work smarter, not harder. Make a market list, prioritize and choose jobs that take you out of the same old routine and develop in you the creativity and flexibility necessary

to keep up with the changes in your community and keep your love of music alive.

12
Contact People
How to make initial contact, and then *keep* in contact, with the potential clients: booking agents, convention planners, caterers, wedding consultants, operators of businesses large and small, public relations and advertising agencies, shopping malls, fashion shows, and clubs . . . and that's only the beginning!

13
More Market Research
Stay aware of old clients' new needs. Research upcoming community events in newspapers and magazines (even the advertisements), chambers of commerce, and library resources.

14
Working With Agents
Establish a good working relationship with your agent—remember he or she is on *your* side. Become a successful, businesslike agent/performer team.

15
Selling
You're not only a musician—you're a salesman, and your product is yourself. So advertise! Get business cards, photos, demo tapes, brochures, flyers, and information sheets. Your first meeting with each potential client is important—prepare for it. Learn to make a persuasive sales presentation. Develop specific sales points to convince customers that you're the one they really want.

16
Pricing and Contracts
Make the price right. Quote too low and the client's apt to be suspicious and not respect you. Quote too high and you'll lose sales. Check out the going rate and the competition. Be realistic. Don't forget your own costs, or your agent's cut. Consider joining a union. Since only amateurs play "for exposure," expect to get paid for what

you do, and always get it in writing. Understand contracts—what does the client expect, what will be provided, what will be paid? What do you promise to do? What happens if you're rained out or the power fails?

17
Playing the Job 165
Often the success of a job depends on nonmusical factors. It's not just how or what you play—it may be whether your shoes are shined or whether you start on time. Little things mean a lot, and the values of the business world don't necessarily parallel those of musicians. Learn the Do's and Don'ts for successful performances that bring clients back a second and third time.

18
The Successful Freelance Musician 169
Practice, practice, practice your profession and never let yourself or your music get stale. The productive freelance music life can be wonderful. You can do what you enjoy—and get paid for it.

Preface

Susan Bennett, a housewife and mother, has a great part-time job. It's easy, fun, and profitable. Most weeks, she makes two to three hundred dollars for just a few hours of work.

Her job? She sings with a freelance dance band. "It's great," she says, "to get out of the household routine, have fun making music, *and* get paid for it."

Allen Stone is a computer programmer for a large company. Many weeks he makes as much money in a few nights, by playing bass with a pop-rock band, as he does in a week on his regular job. Furthermore, he usually works only three or four hours a night.

Brenda Malone is a harpist who plays mostly classical music. She teaches part time in a local junior college, has a few private students, plays several nights every week in an elegant restaurant, and frequently performs for private parties and receptions. She makes a good living from her full-time music career, though she doesn't have a "regular" job, and she enjoys the variety and stimulation of working in different settings.

Susan, Allen, and Brenda are profiting from the freelance music marketplace. Like thousands of other performers, they work an interesting variety of jobs and make a substantial income from their music.

On an hourly basis, in fact, their incomes often rival those of attorneys, accountants, and other professionals. And, since they enjoy music, it's like getting paid for having fun.

Could you make money with music? Did you play an instrument in high school or college? Do you play in a part-time, amateur band or sing with a barbershop quartet? Do you enjoy playing the piano or guitar to entertain your friends?

Or are you now a professional musician but not working enough jobs, not making enough money? Are you caught in the routine world of clubs and lounges, bored with your music—and depressed by your bank statement? Would you like to broaden your musical market to include some of the high-paying jobs that have eluded you?

This book will show you how to make money—or more money—from your music.

Most people think of nightclubs, concerts, or records as the main sources of income for professional musicians. But this is a very limited view, for there are *hundreds of ways* to profit from your music. Many of these opportunities are one-time, or part-time, events that need freelance musicians who are alert, capable, and available.

Many of the best freelance jobs involve playing for private gatherings that the public never hears about. How do you find such jobs? That's where this book comes in. It discusses nearly a hundred different places to sell your music, and it gives you a system for finding the right jobs for you.

Susan and Allen, as part-time musicians, and Brenda, even as a full-time player, aren't tied down to steady music jobs. They have plenty of free time, and their incomes rival those of professionals in other fields. These three successful musicians have learned how to market their music to get the maximum pay for the minimum time.

You can do the same.

How You Can Make $30,000 a Year as a Musician

Introduction

Why You Need This Book

All freelance musicians ask the same question: How can I find more work and make more money?

That question never goes away. Beginners and established professionals alike seek the answer every day. The answer is really quite simple: Play more jobs, and you'll make more money.

But are there really jobs that need your music?

Yes—*if you know where they are.* And if you know how to book and play these low-visibility, high-profit engagements, you'll maximize your profits. You can make $30,000 a year. Or more. The hardest part is finding jobs that need your music.

How You Can Make $30,000 a Year as a Musician offers a universally applicable system for finding jobs. This book will show you how to establish contact with the very people who *need* your music and will pay for it. You'll learn about hundreds of different markets and you'll discover how to pinpoint those that need *your* particular talents.

This system isn't limited to one kind of music or to one category of musicians. It will work for practically *every* freelance musician, although each player's approach will differ, based on his or her own desires, experience, and talent.

Success in playing music for a living doesn't have to be a matter of luck or of who you know. *How You Can Make $30,000 a Year as a Musician* presents a clear method that—step by step—will help you find more work.

HOW THIS BOOK IS ARRANGED

You will find several kinds of help in *How You Can Make $30,000 a Year as a Musician.* First we'll discuss the general philosophy of freelance music, of selling creativity for money. There are a few crucial ideas here that will help ensure your success. Second, we'll get to the practical aspects of the profession. We'll talk about getting organized and becoming businesslike. Then you'll learn how to methodically assess your talents and use some simple market-research techniques to match those talents to the markets you will discover. The jobs you find with this method will be *yours alone,* targeted to your own abilities and aspirations. Worksheets are provided for you to use in preparing your own marketing plan.

The main focus is on *finding jobs,* and the mechanism you'll use is called the *Personal Music Marketing System* or *PMMS.* Devising your own marketing system will require a little work, but it will be well worth it. If you don't use such a system in today's competitive music market, you'll waste countless hours and lots of effort. *How You Can Make $30,000 a Year as a Musician* will show you how to plan your time and how to focus your energy most effectively. Then you'll learn how to use the market information you've developed to locate and meet potential clients, convince them to hire you, and book and play the job.

Even If You're a Genius

Why should a musician have to use a handbook like this to find jobs? Won't agents or bandleaders do that for you? Won't clients call if they need you?

No, they won't.

There are too many musicians and too few jobs for us to relax for long. Even if you are a certified genius, a child prodigy with perfect pitch and a photographic memory, you'll still have to scramble for jobs.

How You Can Make $30,000 a Year as a Musician shows you a new way to think about yourself and your music—an approach that will help you locate, book, and play jobs that need you.

One main point can be stated simply. Playing the job is *easy.* Finding the job is difficult. That's where *How You Can Make $30,000 a Year as a Musician* comes in; it's a marketing guide.

So you won't find any music in this book—not a single note. You should already know how to play your instrument—or be working on it. The book assumes that you are a competent musician, capable of making good music.

If you need to work on your musical technique, this may not be the book for you—yet. But there are thousands of instructional methods, courses, and books that will help you improve your playing.

What about Fame and Fortune?

Would you like to be on the cover of *People* magazine? How about being featured on MTV?

Let's be honest right at the beginning. This book isn't intended to make you rich and famous. We make no claims that it can make you a star, or a wealthy recording artist, or a fixture of the concert circuit.

Becoming a celebrity is, for some people, a worthwhile goal. If that's your desire, work for it. But remember, becoming a star depends on many factors, most of which are out of your control. Hard work and talent will surely be necessary, but so will good luck, charisma, a healthy economy—and knowing the right people.

So, if you want to be a superstar, by all means read the books, including the ones by fabulously rich celebrities, that purport to show you how to become famous, pick the right manager, agent, road crew, lawyer, and recording company. But realize that only a tiny fraction of those who read such books will ever really profit from their from-the-top advice.

Fewer than 1 percent of all working musicians ever become household names. That leaves more than 99 percent of us to make our living from music in our own communities.

How You Can Make $30,000 a Year as a Musician will show you how to prosper by working more frequently in your community, playing music that you enjoy. If this leads to recording contracts and concert dates, that's great! Most working musicians, however, will never attain fame or fortune. Many don't want to.

Making a good living playing music that you, your client, and your audience enjoy is an enviable, and achievable, goal. Millions of people go to work each day hating every minute of it, and you have a chance to get paid for doing what you like best.

PART TIME AND FULL TIME

This book is for *all* musicians who want to profit—or profit more—from music. That includes full-time professionals and part-time players. Most of the emphasis here is, however, on the harder-to-find part-time freelance jobs. Since most of these jobs aren't performed for the public, they aren't easy to locate and book.

Many of these one-time jobs, however, are the cream of the freelance music world. On an hourly basis, these are among the best-paying opportunities for working musicians.

Sometimes these engagements are called "casuals" or "one-nighters." They exist in virtually every part of the country, and if you really want to maximize your music income you'll try to play as many of these jobs as you can.

Of course we also discuss full-time work for freelance musicians. Lounges, clubs, and such steady employment as teaching, working in stores, and playing with symphony orchestras provide lots of opportunity. But the musical spectrum is much broader than these common opportunities, and our method teaches you to search out the little-known freelance jobs that can increase your income or support your entire musical career.

So, if you're a computer programmer who moonlights as a jazz keyboardist, or a landscape gardener who plays the banjo in a part-time bluegrass band, this book will help you find new places to sell your music. And if you are in a top-forty group that plays six nights a week in local clubs, you'll find many suggestions here for other good-paying outlets for your music so you can earn even more.

It doesn't matter whether you play full time for a living or use music as a part-time—but well-paying—hobby. What does matter is your ability to find jobs that will pay you to perform. Your goal is to fill your calendar with high-quality jobs that will pay you for doing what you like best—making music. This book will show you how.

1

Are You Good Enough?

How good must you be to make money with your music? Perfect? Average? Fair? This is a difficult, but important, question that each musician must answer.

Your musical skills should never stop growing. Like a doctor or lawyer, you practice your profession. As music changes, you have to keep up; you can never relax and assume that you're as good as you should be. No one ever is.

HOW TO TELL IF YOU'RE READY TO MAKE MONEY WITH YOUR MUSIC

Visiting jobs you'd like to be playing. Listen and watch to learn what is involved. Which styles should you know? What tunes seem

5

to be the essential "core repertoire" in that style? Are the other musicians reading music? Could you rely on a fake book (which provides only melody lines and chord symbols) or must you know the music without having charts to work from?

Ask questions. Talk with people who play the kind of engagement you are interested in and get firsthand reports on what is required. Many musical jobs seem more intimidating at first than they really are.

Study the repertoire. If you're going after a job playing classical guitar in an exclusive restaurant, do you know enough music to play three or four hours without repeating? Do you know the numbers that will certainly be requested—"Malagueñea," for example?

Polish your showmanship. If you want to sing with a dance or top-forty band, do you know enough lyrics? Do you know how to work a microphone and relate to the crowd? Is your pitch good? Do you understand the structure of tunes, so you will know when to sing and when to leave space for an instrumental solo? Can you do the same tune several times a night, night after night, without getting bored (or letting your boredom show)?

Learn specialized repertoires. If your target is booking ethnic wedding receptions, are you familiar with all the necessary tunes and tempos? Do you know the music for horas, polkas, tarantellas, merengues, or whatever kind of music the client may want?

Nobody is born knowing all this, but you can learn what you need for the jobs you want to play.

HIGH-TECH LEARNING

Use home audiovisual equipment as a learning tool. Borrow or rent what you don't have. Tape record your playing or singing and listen critically. Don't be oversensitive when you hear yourself, but objectively listen for the most important elements of your performance.

If you're a singer, listen to your pitch and phrasing. If you're a drummer, use a metronome to assess your time—from a performance tape, not a practice session. Flashy solos and the best musical equipment won't help if you rush or drag badly.

Use a video camera to find out how you look, particularly if you're a singer or need to be involved with the audience. A few videotape sessions will clearly reveal any amateurish flaws.

One good way to improve your playing, learn new tunes, and have the chance to play with top professionals is to use play-along records. Such popular series as Music Minus One, Drum Drops, and the Jamie Abersold records (see Appendix C) offer valuable experience at modest cost. If you can't play "Stardust" or "Body and Soul," you'll have a hard time establishing yourself as a capable big-band player, but play-along records can teach you these standard tunes and prepare you well for playing for pay.

Again, nobody's perfect. Keep your perspective by remembering how most pop records are made. Days—or weeks—of overdubbing, adding tracks, and "punching in" to cover mistakes ensure that *every* recording will be flawless. Even classical piano albums have been pieced together from several recording sessions to get the best possible performance. It's not fair to judge your live performance by the contrived perfection of most albums.

LEARNING FROM OTHERS

There are all kinds of music teachers, and they can be a great resource to both beginning and advanced musicians. You'll learn more and save much time if you work with a good teacher.

But finding the right teacher to prepare you for playing *professionally* can be difficult. Learning traditional music and proper technique may not be enough. You may require a teacher who understands your special needs and who can provide comprehensive guidance in the most effective sequence. How do you go about finding someone to help you acquire the skills you need?

First, define exactly what you want to learn. If you simply want to work on technique, or reading, or some standard aspect of your instrument, you'll probably be able to find plenty of capable teachers. If, however, you want to learn current pop styles, jazz abilities, or computer/synthesizer interfacing, you'll have a smaller selection of experts who can assist you.

That goes for improvisation as well. In many nonclassical job situations, the ability to improvise is of utmost importance, yet it's a very difficult—if not impossible—skill to teach. Many excellent improvisers, for example, just "play naturally" and can't tell anyone else how to do it.

Often you will profit by taking lessons from a professional player who is not primarily a teacher. Here, though, you must be sure that the pro knows how to teach and can communicate well. Talk to the best players in your area to get leads on appropriate teachers, and investigate schools devoted to your kind of music.

It is certainly possible to become a master musician all by yourself, but why continue to invent the wheel? Use the experience and specialized knowledge of other musicians to save yourself time and effort. Just be sure that the teacher you choose is the teacher you need.

Again, music is practiced. It's not mastered once and for all. If you're good enough today, you may not be adequate tomorrow unless you continue to work at it. Musicians at the very highest levels always continue to practice and work, and you should too.

KNOWING WHAT'S NEEDED

But exactly how good is good enough for commercial music? These points will help you answer that question:

• Be sure you're good enough to do the job. If you have doubts about your ability don't take the engagement! A poor performance will be long remembered by clients, the audience, and other musicians. If you don't think you can perform at a professional level, don't try. You could do more harm than good, and the money you make just won't be worth the damage to your career.

• On the other hand, don't try to practice until you're perfect or you'll never leave your house. There will always be room for improvement—current tunes to learn, more styles to acquire, or new equipment to master.

• Don't overlook the nonmusical factors that are crucial to freelance success. Sometimes a businesslike attitude and pleasant personality are as important as your playing ability. Even marvelous musicians usually have to be on time and be able to get along with the band, the client, and the audience.

• Knowing what the job requires is also important. How will the music fit the overall plan of the event? What's the big picture? What, really, is needed from the musicians? Virtuosity? Usually not. For most jobs, competent playing will be enough.

Finally, since you're a musician, you will usually be a harsher critic of your playing than your clients will be. As long as you can provide what they need, you're good enough for the job.

2

Why You Need a Job-Finding System

Freelance musicians work on a job-by-job basis and often have no steady employment. They play shows, one-nighters, and a wide range of miscellaneous engagements. Some work five or six nights a week in restaurants or clubs, while others don't want such regular work.

They are part-timers or full-time professionals. They may be teachers, students, carpenters, airline pilots, or symphony players. At one time or another, almost all musicians take freelance jobs, sometimes for extra money, or to survive between steady engagements, or as professional, full-time freelancers.

Freelancing can be financially dangerous because there is no steady income. But it can also be exciting, with new challenges each day. And many full-time freelancers make an excellent living without ever having a steady job.

But we all face the same problem. Finding work.

No matter how good you are or how long you've been a professional, you will have to find clients who are willing to pay you money to perform.

HOW BAD IS IT?

Each year there are more and more events and celebrations that need music. But competition keeps pace. There are already far more players than there are regular salaried jobs, and the musician-to-job ratio gets worse all the time.

Working musicians know that there are more musicians than jobs. But how many more?

Precise figures are hard to find, but the increasing amount of money spent on music and instruments indicates how many people are interested in professional music. In 1973, for example, only 7,000 synthesizers were sold, but in 1983 that number had risen to more than 66,000. The total spent on music, instruments, and accessories in the United States rose from $608,000,000 in 1962 to a staggering $2,207,745,000 in 1982. Interest in music, both amateur and professional, is growing faster than the nation's economy.

The 1984-85 Occupational Outlook Handbook of the U.S. Department of Labor discusses the job outlook in music:

The large number of people desiring to be professional musicians, the lack of formal entry requirements for many types of jobs, and the relatively small number of job openings have resulted in keen competition for jobs.

The report continues:

There are not expected to be openings for all job-seekers, and the keen competition for jobs as a musician is expected to continue. Only the most talented are expected to be able to find regular employment.

But in most cases it takes more than talent to succeed.

Classical Music: Too Much Talent, Too Few Jobs

Established symphonies and opera companies can absorb only a few new classical players and singers each year. Since most symphony players are very career-minded, and since these jobs are difficult to find in the first place, turnover in this area of music is very low.

Nevertheless, colleges and universities, conservatories, private teachers, workshops, and special music programs continue to produce thousands of classical musicians each year.

The question is obvious. Where are all of these excellently trained musicians to work? How can they make money with their music if there are so few full-time jobs?

For Pop Music It's Even Worse

Pop, jazz, country, and rock music attract untold thousands of new performers each year. Since anyone can call himself (or herself, of course) a professional and play for pay, there is no way to know how many part-time musicians there are. However, we all know from experience that the number far exceeds the number of jobs available.

What can freelance musicians do? What steps are necessary to prosper—or even survive?

The job-finding system explained in this book will help you match your talents to jobs that need you, whether you're a classical violinist or a country fiddler. Freelance success requires playing many jobs, and this method is an organized approach that will help you target, book, and play engagements that are right for you.

To be successful, you must be prepared.

LEADER OR SIDEMAN?

Should you organize your own musical group and take the responsibility of being a *leader*? Or should you try only to work for other musicians?

You should probably do both. If you are to profit as a freelance musician, you'll have to work as much as possible. Sometimes this may be as a leader, other times as a sideman. If your instrument is used alone, you should play solo performances as well.

There are four categories of musical work that you should keep in mind as you look for jobs that need your music.

Single performers work alone. The advantage is that you are self-contained, not dependent on anyone else. The disadvantages are that all the responsibility is yours, and you have to keep yourself challenged and interested in your work. Typical singles include pianists, guitarists, strolling violinists, banjo players, and accordionists. If you play the bass or drums, you won't work many singles. Single jobs usually pay more than sideman work but less than leader jobs.

Sideman jobs are those you work as a member of someone else's group. You won't make as much money as the leader does, but neither will you have the responsibility of booking the job and keeping the client happy. Most working musicians often play jobs as sidemen, so you should get to know all the bandleaders and contractors in your area. Even established bands frequently need subs or extra players, so stay in touch. They can't call you if they don't know you.

Leader jobs are the ones you book, organize, and play. When you are the leader, it's your responsibility to be sure that the job goes well and that the client is pleased. In return, the leader makes more money—often twice as much as the sideman. If you're good with people, ambitious, and well organized, you should work toward getting as many leader jobs as possible. Why work for sideman's pay when you could double your profit? Of course, the leader must know how to play the job, understand what is required, and see to it that the engagement goes well.

Contractors are musicians who hire other players but do not necessarily play the job. A contractor is part musician and part agent. Typical work includes hiring musicians for large shows and traveling jobs (such as circuses and ice shows) and handling hiring for out-of-town agencies. For example, a famous entertainer doing a tour of smaller cities in the southwestern states may contract all the needed musicians out of one major city—perhaps Los Angeles—or may use a contractor to pick up local players in each city on the tour.

So, if you are a successful freelance musician, you should be known by those who typically contract large jobs. Also, when you begin to get calls for jobs you can't handle yourself, you can work as a contractor and arrange for other musicians to handle the engagements. Contractors are more common in large cities than in smaller, less busy sites.

EVERYTHING MUST CHANGE

Part of the difficulty in being a freelance musician today is the dynamic nature of American life. Not only must we keep up with changing musical styles and new equipment, but we should also stay abreast of broader changes that affect us all.

The United States is shifting from an industrial to an information-based economy, and the changes are widespread. Some cities and sections of the country will expand dynamically; others will lose population. New industries will appear, and old ones will decline. Entirely new markets for music will emerge, and the freelance player who is prepared will profit. Some examples.

● As computers become more common and personal interaction on the job decreases, the need for human contact will grow. John Naisbitt, in his recent book *Megatrends,* calls this "high tech/high touch." For musicians, one outcome may be that the human interaction of the live dance band won't be displaced by the sterility of the disco—no matter what the quality of the music. People enjoy interacting with *people*—not machines.

● Leisure time will continue to expand. Music teachers, for example, will have more students, especially for the most popular instruments (which are, in order, piano, guitar, organ, clarinet, drums, flute, trumpet).

● Electronic advances will continue to make sophisticated recording technology available to smaller and smaller communities. For musicians, work in recording studios will no longer be limited to New York, Los Angeles, and Nashville. Just a few years ago, good recording equipment was too expensive for small businesses, but now many small cities boast several high-quality studios, giving work to local writers, producers, players, singers, technicians, and engineers.

YOU NEED A SYSTEM

You can succeed in music—even though there are more players than jobs—*if you know how.*

What real difference does it make to you if there are too many players? What if there are too few jobs? You don't have to succumb to statistics. All you really need to do is find enough jobs for yourself or your group. But—how do you do that?

The answer is to use a *job-finding system*. The one that's described in this book is called the *Personal Music Marketing System* (PMMS); I know it works because I use it. You may devise another method that works as well for you, and if so, that's great—use it and prosper.

Realize, though, that the music business is not an easy place to make a lot of money with little effort. If you're lazy and just wait for your phone to ring, you may manage to survive—but that's about all you'll do.

On the other hand, if you use a system and apply it energetically, you'll find jobs where you didn't see them before, and you'll provide the kind of music your audience and clients need. You'll be in demand. You'll know the secrets of musical success—but they aren't really secrets. They are explained in this book. All you have to do is put them into use.

Practice makes perfect, but your Personal Music Marketing System will make money.

3

The Basic Idea: Music Is a Product

Music, like soap, is a product. It is produced, marketed, and sold, and you should understand this process if you want to make money with your music. Those who aren't comfortable with this state of affairs will sit at home on Saturday nights and wonder why they never work.

To be successful making money from music, the musicians must also know that music is a business. This concept is as true for classical players and symphony orchestras as it is for country singers and rock bands. It applies even to religious music.

We'll call this the "reality" of commercial music. It may not be what you'd like to believe, or what your professors taught, but when you try to make money by playing music, you'll have to face the facts of the marketplace.

HE WHO PAYS THE PIPER
CALLS THE TUNE

The reality is that clients buy only what they need or want. Your clients will buy your music only because it will do something for them. It may entertain them, help celebrate an event, create a special mood, or simply demonstrate their affluence. But in every instance they will pay for music because it's what they need.

Rarely, or never, will you be hired just to play your own music in your own way. To be successful, you must find out what your potential clients require and be able to fulfill that need.

Your music is a service to those who hire you, and it must satisfy them to justify its cost. Your clients usually won't be philanthropists; they aren't interested in supporting struggling artists.

To compete successfully in commercial music, then, you must follow the same strategy that every successful businessperson uses.

Develop a product—in this case, your music.

Locate clients for your product. Do market research.

Bring your product to the marketplace. Use sales ability to convince potential clients to buy your music.

Most musicians see themselves, rightly, as artists and to many of them treating music as a product seems heretical. But if you intend to make money from your music, you can't afford to feel that way.

Your music must serve a purpose for clients, or it is a waste of their money. Your job, if you make money from music, is to learn what clients need and how to fulfill their needs.

Balancing Beauty and the Business

Does this mean that to succeed in commercial music you'll have to "sell out"? No. Successful musicians don't need to be hacks, and they certainly don't have to reject the artistry and beauty of music.

You must develop a salable product, but this is only part of your art. Your clients buy only a little of your music for a short time. They don't own your life. Play what your clients need, if you can, but remember that your musical life is broader than any job situation.

If you plan to make money with your music, you'll have to balance the needs of your clients against your musical preferences. Most likely, you will know more about music than your clients—that's your job—but they know what they want. And they sign the checks.

Every profession has its tradeoffs, and heeding customers' preferences is one of ours. If you simply can't bring yourself to play what the job requires, then don't take it. *For some players, music is better as a hobby than as a career.*

So, does success in commercial music mean playing music that you don't like, perhaps even music of dubious quality? Yes, sometimes.

This kind of compromise is common in other professions, too. A dentist might hate doing root canals, but he or she probably does them because that's part of the job, and the dentist is in it, ultimately, for the money. An English teacher may hate teaching grammar, but if it's part of the curriculum, it goes with the position. Almost every job that pays money has some disagreeable aspects, whether it's doing root canals, teaching grammar, or playing "In the Mood" or "Claire de Lune" for the ten-thousandth time.

Every musician, especially freelancers who work in a variety of situations, must decide where to draw the musical line. Each player must decide how "commercial" to be. There is no need to try constantly to play music you hate; both you and your client will be dissatisfied. Sometimes it boils down to how far you can compromise without making yourself miserable.

PROFESSIONAL PLEASURE

There is another kind of musical pleasure you may come to enjoy—the satisfaction of "the professional job well done." You may find that playing only the kind of music you like is not as important to you as doing what the job at hand requires. Pleasing the client can be the ultimate measure of success.

Often there is a challenge in figuring out exactly what your client needs and fulfilling that need, regardless of what it is and regardless of how much you like that kind of music. A carpenter may prefer to build only modern cedar-and-glass houses, but a real sense of personal satisfaction can result from meeting the challenge of restoring an old Victorian mansion.

Similarly, you may reach the point where you enjoy—*really enjoy*—making your clients happy with your music, even when what they want isn't what you'd prefer to play. That's what it means to be a professional. When you reach that level, you're on your way to success as a freelance musician.

THE BOTTOM LINE

Music must serve a need for the consumer—or there is no need for the music.

James Goodfriend, writing in *Stereo Review* (July 1982), makes this point clearly: "In the business of music, the quality of the work is not at all the central point. That central point is whether enough people will like it . . . to pay for it."

This is equally true for the nightclub owner who hires "personality" rather than talent and for the symphony conductor who schedules programs that will draw large crowds—and pay the bills.

Analyze the needs of the marketplace, fill those needs, and you'll be successful.

4

Music Is a Business

You may be an incredible musician, but that's not enough to make you successful. To make money you'll have to sell your music, and to do that you'll need to be businesslike and organized.

Organization is not the opposite of creativity. Organization can give you more time to be creative. Your own music business most likely won't succeed unless you are organized.

Being a successful musician is a lot more complicated than it might seem at first. You are a musician, of course, but you are also a part-time salesperson, advertising specialist, secretary, accountant, sound engineer, equipment mover, and much more. You'll have less trouble balancing these various tasks if you stay organized, and that's not as hard as you might think.

If you rely on your memory, correspondence and contracts piled haphazardly on your desk, or important notes scribbled on bits of paper, you'll soon be in trouble. You'll forget important requirements and requests, double-book yourself, hire three drummers for the same job, or even miss engagements. This will quickly lead to a reputation for unreliability that will stop your career before it gets started.

You'll also save a lot of time—your most valuable commodity—if you stay organized. Every time you waste fifteen minutes looking for a misplaced contract you have lost a quarter of an hour that could have been used productively.

Here are some ideas that will help. Keep them in mind while you work on your marketing system, and as you book more and more jobs, you'll be in control of the information that you'll need.

GETTING ORGANIZED

As you develop your Personal Music Marketing System, you'll need to keep lots of information neatly at hand. Information is important in our job-finding system, and a simple filing system will supplement your memory. This does not mean scraps of paper stuffed in your pocket or filed in your wallet.

The Personal Music Marketing System discussed in this book will only work if you actually make the suggested lists and *write them down*. It won't work if you just think about it. To keep your lists and brainstorming ideas handy, you should use a notebook or loose-leaf binder. Information is essential to this system, and if you keep it in one place, you'll be able to find it when you need it. If you prefer, use the worksheets provided here, or photocopy them for use in your notebook.

A three-ring loose-leaf binder, with paper and subject dividers, is a good start. Or use a file folder for each possible client to keep all related information together. If you don't have a filing cabinet, use a cardboard box. When you work lots of jobs, you'll never remember all the details; if you file the details, you won't have to worry.

A datebook is also necessary. Be sure to get one that allows plenty of room for making notes. If your kind of musical enterprise requires a lot of weekend work, be sure that Saturdays and Sundays are given equal space with weekdays in whatever datebook you use. One popular brand is the Week at a Glance series that most office-supply stores have. This will be your nerve center and will tell you where to go and when to be there. Don't lose it.

A pocket notebook will also be useful. One of the techniques you'll use in developing your *PMMS* will be brainstorming, and you'll get all kinds of ideas—possible clients, job leads, public-relations thoughts, songs to learn—all the time.

An expense-record book such as the Dome 700 (about $3), will pay for itself many times over in tax savings. Remember that you are a businessperson as well as a musician, and every tax deduction and business expense that you can document will be money in your pocket.

Tickle Your Memory

You can't rely on memory alone to direct all the complicated details of your freelance music career. Will you really remember to write that follow-up letter, keep that important appointment, or mail those contracts? And how will you remember to call someone who won't be back from vacation for three more weeks?

Freelance musicians, like business executives and sales representatives, have innumerable appointments to keep, tasks to perform, and important details to follow up. They need—*you need*—a systematic way of scheduling activities and making sure those activities are carried out—on time.

What's the solution? A *tickler file* to augment your datebook.

Systems to tickle or jog your memory are abundant in office-supply stores, but you can devise your own at less expense. Set up a file folder for each month and enter chronologically the details of things to be done. Cross reference or cue the entries to your datebook.

Thus, your datebook for June 6 might read, "Letter to Acme Co." Referring to your June tickler file, you would find the notations "June 6: sales promotion material to Acme Co. re Christmas party. To Bill Smith, Ass't VP. Had 7-piece band last year. Budget around $1,000. Lots of top-40." The address and other pertinent notes follow.

After you mail that letter to Mr. Smith at Acme, note in your datebook and tickler file that three or four weeks later—say July 1—you should follow up this letter if need be. In the tickler file be sure to mention the date of the original letter so that you can locate it quickly for reference.

Another simple tickler system uses three-by-five-inch index cards, with monthly dividers. (If you're really busy, you could set up a card system with a card for each day of the year.) Each card contains information about one job, client, or whatever, and the cards are filed chronologically.

Whichever system you use—perhaps you'll invent your own—make it as foolproof as you can. This means that you must think of some method for ensuring that you *refer to your datebook and tickler file every day.* It's a great system for freeing your mind from annoying details, but it won't work unless you use it.

Knowing What's Important

Part of being organized is knowing what information is important and what's not. What should you ask? What should you save? What should you write down, and what should you try to remember?

As you sell your music to many clients, you will quickly learn that you can't rely on your memory alone. Did Mr. Jones hate rock and roll, or was it Mr. Smith? Did the Pines Country Club want the band to start at seven o'clock or eight? Should you use the service entrance or the front door at the Seabreeze Resort? What is the client's favorite song?

This is obviously the kind of information you'll want to write down. Keep it in your datebook if there's enough space or in a clearly labeled file folder.

Also keep up with all the incidental information that will be part of your marketing (and musical) activities. When a client has a birthday, or mentions a favorite tune, or has a new baby, make a note to use this information for adding a personal touch to your business relationship.

If you subscribe to magazines or journals—and all musicians should—you may want to establish a clip file of interesting articles. A large stack of magazines is virtually useless, but an organized file of helpful articles can be a gold mine of ideas.

KNOWING WHO'S IMPORTANT

The music business—like all others—revolves around who you know. Your network of contacts, acquaintances, and friends of friends is crucial to your success. You'll need to know as many musicians, agents, and possible clients as you can—not to mention secretaries and office-staff members. Here are a few suggestions for knowing—and remembering—who's important.

- Who's important to your musical life? Potentially, almost everybody you meet, so you should always keep your own business cards handy and be alert for possible clients wherever you go. (Business cards and other promotional strategies will be covered in Chapter 15, "Selling.")

• Your music career will be as much a "people business" as a musical enterprise, so cultivate your social skills. One of the most important is the ability to remember names and faces, and this isn't as hard as it may seem. Read a book on improving your memory (such as *Stop Forgetting* by Bruno Furst—see Appendix B), and use the recommended techniques. People are flattered when you remember their names and may be offended when you don't. Many successful piano-bar entertainers have prodigious memories for regular customers' names and favorite songs.

• To aid your memory, buy a business-card file at an office-supply store. Ask for cards from possible clients, musicians you meet, and other contacts. Jot down pertinent information on the back of each card—such as where and when you met and what you talked about. File business cards alphabetically by name or by subject—that is, under "agents," "drummers," "potential clients," "established clients," and so on.

• Establish a "Names to Remember/Contact People" file, and keep information in it about the people you need to stay in touch with. This expanded version of your business-card file will contain entries like "Janice Traylor, catering mgr at new Marriott. Met 9/17/85 at Smith wedding. Needs music frequently. Has new baby. Secy's name: Sandra Underwood." Next time you call on Janice Traylor, you'll be able to recall these personal items and keep your relationship moving. Update this file each time you contact people; that "new baby" will grow up fast, and secretaries move on.

Networking is a fashionable term for using personal or business contacts to further a cause or a career. Whether you call it networking or "being friendly," you'll find that one good contact leads to another. People—not the best musical instruments or the ability to play a pentatonic scale at dazzling speed—are the lifeblood of your profession.

One idea is to throw an occasional party—maybe on Sunday afternoon—and invite other musicians, bandleaders, agents, party planners, and as many other potential clients as you can. You'll have a chance to meet people in your field, expand your network of contacts, and maybe even make a little music. And, if you plan such a party as a business-oriented function, it's tax deductible.

THE TELEPHONE—YOUR LIFELINE

The telephone will be your lifeline. You'll use it to approach clients, book jobs, hire other musicians, and follow up after engagements. You'll spend a lot of time on the phone, so keep up with the changing technology.

You'll probably find that phone calls come in clusters at certain times—often around nine in the morning, at noon, and just before five o'clock. If your clients get a busy signal, they may give up and hire someone else. For a few dollars a month, most phone companies offer a call waiting service that will allow you to put a second incoming call on hold. This is a valuable service for anyone who does a lot of telephoning—as you will.

Now that most customers own their own telephone equipment, all kinds of useful devices are reaching the market. You may find such items as cordless phones, automatic memory dialers, or speaker-phones to be of great value.

One thing is certain. You, as a successful freelance musician, will be spending lots of time on the telephone, so you should make it as efficient and helpful a tool as you can.

Don't forget that, when used for business, telephone-equipment purchase and operating costs are tax deductible.

Answering Services and Machines

You'll probably need some kind of answering service—either human or electronic. It's pleasing to have a real person answer the phone, and answering services do. They're expensive, however, and a grouchy or forgetful operator can quickly ruin the human advantage.

Answering machines are almost universally accepted now, and most people, whether they like to or not, will leave messages. Before buying an answering machine, shop around and compare prices and features. Here are some important considerations:

- *Is the machine battery or AC operated? Batteries run down, need replacing, and are more expensive in the long run. Plug-in machines are better.*

- *Will the machine take only thirty-second messages, or is it voice actuated to record as long as your caller talks? Voice-actuated machines won't cut the caller off in midsentence.*

- *Is there a remote beeper or other electronic method that will allow you to get your messages from another telephone? This is a very useful feature.*

- *Can you change the tapes yourself? Some machines rely on built-in tapes that can't be replaced by the user. Others use simple cassettes that can be easily changed.*

- *When will the machine answer? Some machines will pick up only at a preselected ring—the second, for example. Others allow the user to set the machine to answer on any given ring. This is a very handy option.*

- *Can you vary the length of your outgoing message? Sometimes you won't have much to say; other times you will.*

- *Is local repair service available? Every machine will eventually need it, and shipping your unit back to the manufacturer could be inconvenient.*

Consider these features before you spend your money. A few more dollars spent to get a good, well-built machine with useful features will serve you well over the years you'll use it.

WORKING IS TAXING

You work hard to make money with your music, and you must work to keep as much of it as you can. In fact, time spent in tax planning may be more profitable to you on an hourly basis than the time you spend making the money.

Needless to say, save every receipt that could possibly document a tax deduction. Keep neat records of your music income and expenses in ink, in a permanently bound ledger. The IRS is suspicious of loose-leaf expense records.

Typical business expenses for musicians include equipment purchases and repairs, travel expenses, music and record purchases (when used for business), and magazine and professional-journal subscriptions. Sales-related costs—such as printing, photography, demo tape production, and phone calls—are also deductible.

Actually, any expenses directly related to your business may be deductible, including the cost of your home office, *but these expenses must be well documented.* Consult an accountant, read a tax-preparation book, and get in the habit of recording *every* business cost as you incur it. Even twenty-five-cent phone calls add up.

Should you—a working freelance musician—really use an accountant? Yes. An accountant's services should save you more than they cost, and they may keep you out of tax trouble as well. Don't try to use the large, most prestigious accounting firms, however, and steer clear of the seasonal storefront or part-time tax-return preparers. While your tax situation may be complex to you, it will be simple to a professional tax advisor. An independent accountant can give you expert advice, figure deductions, compile depreciation, prepare your returns, and generally help lower your tax liability.

You must also know the tax laws concerning subcontractors and who should be sent a 1099 or W2 form. If you pay another musician more than $600 a year for working with you, you must submit one of these forms in January of the following year. *Form 1099* is sent to subcontractors, making them responsible for paying their own taxes. The *W-2 form* is similar but involves the complications of figuring withholding rates, subtracting taxes from payments, and sending those taxes to the IRS. Get an accountant's advice on which to use.

If you pay out substantial sums to other musicians, it is very important to send 1099 or W-2 forms. Otherwise, the IRS might require you to pay taxes on money you actually paid to someone else. A trumpet player in Atlanta, who was audited in 1985, was assessed $10,000, including penalties and interest, for failing to document his 1982 freelance-musician payroll. Don't let this happen to you.

You have to pay taxes, but you don't have to pay more than you owe. Know current tax requirements, keep your records up to date, and get professional help.

The amount of information we need to be successful increases yearly. We are living in the "information age." Often, what, and who, you know will be as important as what you do. The successful musician is the one who will work to stay organized and will know where to find information when it's needed.

5

Developing Your Personal Music-Marketing System

Music is different from many other professions in one important way. Experienced working musicians and beginners alike face the same recurring, all-important question: How can I work more jobs? That remains the bottom line for both newcomers and established professionals. But just waiting for the telephone to ring with job offers is unnecessarily depressing.

So is just playing the same old jobs with the same group of musicians. Nothing is worse than a bad habit, and freelancers must work to stay fresh and interested. We've all seen tired, burned-out players who look too bored to hold their horns. It's better to leave the profession than to end up this way. Fortunately, there are alternatives.

The system described in this book will help you deal positively with these problems. It offers every musician an easy, organized, and personalized way to find more jobs. There's nothing complex or revolutionary about this system. In fact, it works *because* it is simple.

29

As music changes and your community grows, the job market will change and expand. This system will help you stay current, and staying current will help keep you interested—and interesting.

THE BASIC IDEA

The next chapters of *How You Can Make $30,000 a Year as a Musician* explain a method that can help you systematically locate the kinds of music jobs that will best suit your talents and interests.

If you do the brainstorming and research, if you make the lists that are the basis of the system, you will discover lots of job opportunities in your own area, and you'll have a valuable, personalized source of information that will make it easier for you to book and play engagements.

The basic idea of the marketing system is to match your own abilities with jobs that call for your kind of music. This is done in several steps.

● Assess and list your own musical skills, abilities, and equipment. This will be your Personal Inventory list.

● Compile a list of every single kind of music job that might—even remotely—need your services. Then match your skills to the jobs that require them and develop a Job Possibilities list.

● When that is well under way, you'll refine it to get a working list of Best Possibilities. This will guide your initial marketing plans.

● Expand your best possibilities list to include the names and addresses of contact people. This will be your Good Prospects list, and these people will become your clients.

Each of these steps will be explained in detail later. You'll find it easy to create *your own* marketing system as you read on.

Again, it's necessary to *write down the information you compile* and really make your lists. Worksheets are provided in this book, but if you can't or don't want to write in the book, use a notebook to keep all this information together. You can't trust your memory—the system will only work if you write it down, and keeping all the lists, worksheets, and brainstorming ideas in one place will save you time and effort.

Everyone Is Different

The spectrum of musical styles, types, and needs is incredibly broad. It simply isn't possible to be a jack-of-all-trades musician; some specialization is required. Rock players usually don't play classical music, and jazz musicians don't generally know country tunes.

Of course, if your abilities cover more than one category, your chances for employment are multiplied. No matter, though, how versatile you are, it's not likely that you can do everything. You'll need to target your markets to match your musical specialties.

Your PMMS will guide you in the effective use of your energy and time. It will direct you to clients who will be receptive because they need what you have to offer, and it will make your sales calls easier. Your Good Prospects list will be different from any other musician's list because it will be based on your abilities and targeted to likely clients in *your community*. It is a precise marketing tool because it is tailored by you—for you.

BRAINSTORMING

Before you can sell your music, you need to define your target clients, and you'll use several steps and methods to locate them. One of the best methods for generating new ideas in developing your PMMS is called *brainstorming*. We all sink into mental ruts or habits of thinking that limit our lives. Brainstorming frees the mind to come up with novel approaches. It's a mental exercise.

Brainstorming is a way to break down old habits and open your mind to fresh ideas and insights. It's an antidote to mental stagnation.

Here's how to brainstorm:

Find a good place to think, where you won't be interrupted—perhaps your local library, or a park bench, or even driving along the interstate highway (in which case you'd use a tape recorder instead of a notebook).

Try to put your mind in "neutral." Let it coast without conscious direction, and follow it wherever it goes. You'll use your memory and imagination, but you won't know where they're taking you. Don't worry. Brainstorming will lead you to new ideas.

Think about your subject—potential clients or possible playing engagements, for example—and write down every single idea that pops into your head, no matter how unlikely, foolish, or absurd it might seem at first. Paper is cheap, and you are trying to generate new ideas, so don't hold back.

Let one idea lead to another. Let your mind roam as far as possible, and let your imagination take over. Don't worry about being practical. That is exactly what brainstorming tries to overcome.

When you are brainstorming, for example, in a search for new job possibilities, try to make your lists as long and full as you can. No one needs to see them except you, so don't hesitate to follow your unconscious mind as it creates ideas.

Be imaginative. Be ridiculous, but don't feel ridiculous. Be as free and open as possible. Imagine your brass ensemble playing at the governor's mansion, or your fifties show entertaining on a Caribbean cruise ship. Bypass the ordinary, leap over the usual and mundane. You'll edit your lists later, but at first just try to come up with new ideas. Don't try to be realistic at all. Just think freely and add to your lists!

Expand your lists through *association*. That is, let one idea lead naturally to a similar one. When your mind is coasting in neutral, ideas will automatically suggest others, link themselves together, and lead to even more new thoughts. If you've thought of playing exciting music for the introduction of next year's new car models, *association* leads you to think of doing the same thing for next year's new speedboats, fur coats, computers, or swimsuits. One idea leads directly—or indirectly—to another, and the more you free your mind from its habits, the more creative it will be.

Perhaps your brainstorming leads you to a client whom you hadn't thought of before, a client who will need your musical services just once a year. That's good.

If, through more brainstorming, association, and research, you can find fifty once-a-year clients, you will have discovered almost a job a week. That's significant.

So don't worry if an idea seems simple, even trivial. Add it to your list anyhow. Careers can be built of many simple ideas.

Always keep your pocket notebook ready for insights, names, or interesting information so that your musical employment possibilities will continue to expand. Once you start thinking in this open-minded way, you'll be constantly alert for new ideas and job possibilities. Adding to and modifying the lists that form your PMMS will be an ongoing process, a never-finished project that will grow with your music life and the changes in your community.

The More You Put into Your PMMS . . .

The PMMS may sound like a lot of work—and it will take a good deal of time—but your preparatory work will pay off handsomely. Each client you discover and cultivate will remember you in the future, and your bank balance will grow with each job you play. Better yet, each job can lead to several others, so your list of clients and contacts will grow geometrically—until you have more work than you can handle. Thus, the work you put into developing this marketing system will be repaid in dollars, new friendships, and feelings of satisfaction for years to come.

If you really want more and more jobs, this system will get you started, and the more work you put into it, the more helpful it will be.

6

Your Personal Inventory

The first list in the PMMS is a compilation of all the musical things you can do that might be salable. Notice that I said "might," because you shouldn't worry about being practical at this point. If you know everything Gilbert and Sullivan wrote, put light opera on your list—even if you don't know of a single job that needs this specialty. Market research comes later. To be useful, your inventory list must be specific and as complete as you can make it.

The Personal Inventory has three parts: a listing of your musical strengths, a listing of your equipment, and a ranking of your abilities.

Please note that this list is not only to be a compilation of the jobs you are now playing or have played. It's to be a list of what you could play now and what you might be able to play in the future. Don't be limited by your past.

FIRST, COMPILE YOUR LIST OF PERSONAL MUSICAL STRENGTHS

The first part of your personal inventory, then, is a summary of what you do best, your musical strengths. To begin, use the Personal Music Inventory Worksheet on page 39 and list everything musical that you can do. Use extra paper if you need it. *The system won't work unless you actually write this information down. You can't do it in your head.*

Don't worry yet about how good you are. Just write down everything that you have done and would like to do in music. Use your memory and your imagination.

To jog your memory and encourage you to break out of your playing habits, the worksheet is divided into several categories. They are:

Kinds of music I can play. Here, you'll list everything musical you now do at a professional, or near-pro, level. This part of your list will be the easiest to compile, since you'll list what you already know and do.

Kinds of music I'd like to play. List here the things you could do with a little work. Also list your long-term playing goals, to show where you'd like to go. If there's a style you haven't mastered, or a composer whose work you don't yet know, this is the place to list it.

Kinds of music I've played in the past. Think back to your earlier playing experiences and school days. List whatever musical activities you used to do. Did you play trumpet in the band? Were you the accompanist for the men's chorus? Did you play harmonica in a blues band that only performed in your garage? Don't reject anything because you haven't done it lately. Think back, and add to your list.

Kinds of music I could play—but don't enjoy. This could be the most important part of your list, because you may find that what the market needs is not exactly your favorite kind of music. Think about the commercially useful types of music that you could do, and add those categories to this part of your list. It doesn't mean that you *have* to play music you don't like, but you need a complete picture of the entire music market to make your system work.

Here's an example. Let's say that you're a freelance keyboard player. Let's assume that you have some classical piano background and that you are able to play a variety of jobs on piano, electric piano, and synthesizer. We'll say that you're mostly interested in pop and rock but can play in other styles with some ease. Further, you played trumpet in the high school band and sang in college theatrical productions.

The first list in your Personal Inventory might look like this—in no particular order:

Personal Music Inventory List

Kinds of Music I can Play
Pop, contemporary
Pop, middle of the road
Rock
Disco

Kinds of Music I'd Like to Play
Jazz
Recording, jingles, demos, etc.
Shows
Teaching

Kinds of Music I've Played in the Past
Classical
Accompanying, classical instrumental
Accompanying, vocal
Church music, organ
Trumpet work, from high school band
Vocal work, from college theater experience

Kinds of Music I Could Play—but Don't Enjoy
Country
Solo work
Big-band work
Ragtime
Sing along

Such a list would be a good starting point for a well-rounded pianist. Notice that this list only notes types of music—without ranking ability or the job prospects in each field. Some pianists can compile longer lists—more specialties, more categories.

Again, don't be concerned if your abilities are not equally developed in all parts of your inventory. Every player will be much stronger in some areas than in others.

As you work on your musical inventory, remember: You don't have to be a virtuoso to make money from music. You may excel in one rather narrow field—sacred organ music, sing-along piano, or bluegrass banjo, for example. Don't worry, therefore, if this first list is short. You can still market your music to a select group of clients.

Don't Rank—Just List!

At this point, make no attempt to rank your talents. That will come later. Obviously, in our example, the pianist won't be as adept at classical music as at disco, or vice versa, but that's not important. What is important is defining and developing your salable skills. You are not listing only your outstanding talents or your virtuoso abilities. You are listing everything you might want to do in music along with everything you have done or can do. Later you will concentrate on what is salable.

To help make your inventory list as inclusive as possible, think about:

Composers. Perhaps listing the composers you're familiar with will suggest certain types of music to you.

Instruments. Thinking about all the instruments you play may suggest more possibilities for your list. If you play trumpet, does your list also include music associated with cornet, piccolo trumpet, valve trombone? If you play piano, think—for your list—about music you could perform on organ, synthesizer, harpsichord, or accordion.

Use brainstorming techniques to think of musical talents that you don't normally use. Try to break out of your old thinking patterns as you compile this list.

PERSONAL INVENTORY WORKSHEET

Kinds of Music I Can Play _____

Kinds of Music I'd Like to Play _____

Kinds of Music I've Played in the Past _____

Kinds of Music I Could Play—but Don't Enjoy _____

ARE YOU FULLY EQUIPPED?

The second part of your Personal Inventory will be a list of all the equipment you own. Use the worksheet shown on page 41. Include what's in your closet or attic as well as what you commonly use. If you are a guitarist, for example, don't forget other stringed instruments that you own—banjo, lute, mandolin, twelve-string, and so on. An occasional show or recording session might call for lute, and if you can play the part, why not collect the pay? Though you may never make a living as a lutist, an occasional job could be significant. Don't overlook any possibilities.

If you own equipment that you can't play, what should you do?

Learn to play it, if that's feasible. The more you can do, the more valuable you are. Don't spread yourself too thin, though. Don't take time away from important piano practice or from marketing your music to learn to play an old guitar you found in the attic.

Keep it, if there is some advantage in doing so. Maybe you can rent that tuba, synthesizer, or sound system even if you don't use it yourself. Or maybe your children will someday take violin lessons. Perhaps the instrument you own, but can't play, is a family heirloom or a potentially valuable antique.

Sell it. If you don't need it, get rid of it. There is no reason to store, maintain, keep up with, and insure musical instruments that are of no practical use to you. You're a musician, not a junk dealer.

It is helpful to see in black and white exactly what you have; the list will help define the variety of jobs you are prepared to play.

Maybe a new piece of equipment would fill a gap or improve your performance—a new microphone, say, or a state-of-the-art synthesizer. Is there an area where you need backup instruments or accessories? If your livelihood depends on an electric bass, shouldn't you have an extra one—just in case?

You may be astonished at the total value of your equipment once you see it listed. Be sure you have proper insurance. Expensive instruments can disappear in a flash or easily be damaged. Insurance is almost always worth its cost.

You may be able to add a "floater" to your household or renter's insurance to cover your instruments, or you may have to buy a separate

EQUIPMENT INVENTORY WORKSHEET

Equipment	Model #	Serial #	Date Purchased	Place Purchased	Cost

policy. Some musicians may need a small businessowner's package to cover not only instruments but office equipment and car as well. Talk with several insurance agents to get a good overview of what's available.

Of course you're careful with your instruments, but you can't guard them twenty-four hours a day. No matter what your instrument, it can be stolen, damaged, or lost. A reed player, for example, who has piccolo, flutes, clarinets, alto, tenor, and baritone saxes, and perhaps an oboe or English horn has a huge investment—even if the instruments are only student models. If you don't have insurance, get it.

NOW PUT THEM IN ORDER

Wait a few days and then read over your Personal Inventory lists. Add anything that you originally overlooked. Then loosely rank your entries using the worksheet on page 43 or your notebook. Use general categories such as "excellent," "fair," and "needs work." Remember that if you are proficient at a style you don't particularly like, it should still be near the top of your list. And of course, if you enjoy another style that you don't really play very well, it should be ranked lower.

You may be surprised at your own musical strengths, and you'll probably find a few other areas that, with a little work, could be salable.

Here's how the pianist in our example might rank the items from her Personal Music Inventory List. Notice that her rankings do not correspond exactly with the categories on the inventory worksheet.

Personal Ranking
1. *Rock—excellent.*
2. *Pop, contemporary—excellent, know all current tunes.*
3. *Disco—excellent, good synth technique.*
4. *Solo piano—good, but don't enjoy working alone.*
5. *Country—fair, know more standards than newer tunes. Don't particularly like this style. Easy for me to improve here.*
6. *Big band ('30s, '40s, '50s)—pretty good but know few tunes.*
7. *Jazz—good, fair repertory, especially '50s, '60s, and '70s standards. Weaker on contemporary tunes.*
8. *Ragtime/boogie-woogie/sing-along—fair, don't enjoy these styles very much, know few tunes.*

9. *Accompanying—good with pop, fair with classical.*

10. *Classical—fair, poor repertoire. Rarely play, but could be 100% better with just a little work.*

11. *Church organ playing—weak because of years of neglect. Could improve quickly with practice.*

12. *Recording studio—little experience, but could quickly improve. Competent with many styles, good reader—should pursue this.*

13. *Show playing—fair with low-pressure shows, could improve with experience.*

14. *Teaching—don't know, never tried, might be a good teacher. Should look into this possibility for daytime income.*

15. *Trumpet work—would take more practice time than I can allow. Not really commercially useful talent without lots of work.*

16. *Vocal work—weak, but could improve with practice and confidence. Might really improve commercial prospects if I knew tunes and sang with confidence.*

Every single item on the list won't deserve your time: Some styles may already be good enough, and others aren't worth the effort required to bring them up to professional quality. In this example trumpet playing may not be a realistic market for our keyboard player, but she might decide to work on the others to bring them up to a salable level.

USING THIS INFORMATION

In this example, notice the categories that our pianist has placed toward the bottom of her list—sing along, organ playing, vocal work, and teaching. She could, with a little work, make these areas more commercially valuable.

PERSONAL INVENTORY RANKING WORKSHEET

Excellent _____

Fair _____

Need Work _____

Pay particular attention, then, to the bottom third of your list, areas that you don't particularly enjoy doing or haven't yet mastered. Here's where, with a bit of work, you might be able to double or triple your salable music skills.

Why? Because you've probably spent most of your time working on the kind of music you like. That's normal. Maybe the intricacies of contemporary jazz fascinate you and you spend hours perfecting stunning solos—and this skill will probably be at the top of your list. But unfortunately there will usually be more jobs available using the skills you ranked lower. Dance work, big-band engagements, even dixieland playing will be more commercially valuable than "pure" jazz. The marketplace isn't as musically sophisticated as you are.

This is a hard lesson to learn, but it is part of facing the reality of the music market. So look carefully at items on the lower part of your list to find untapped commercial potential.

Think Like General Foods

One common business practice is to survey the market to see what is needed and then develop a product to meet those needs. If General Foods, through market research, discovers a market for a breakfast cereal shaped like the space shuttle, you can bet that it will be in the supermarkets shortly.

You can apply the same idea to your music. If, later on, you find that there are lots of music jobs in one particular area, you may decide to become proficient in that category because you know that's what the market needs—and will support.

If, then, as you complete your market lists, you discover several job possibilities in your weaker areas, it might be wise to practice, or woodshed, a bit to bring these areas up to a salable level. That's using the big-business approach: develop a product for an existing market.

You don't have to be in love with a style of music to make money with it. You may find that you enjoy getting paid for playing sing-along jobs, even if you don't particularly like playing that style of music.

Keep in Mind . . .

No one else needs to see your lists, so be honest—but also be creative and inclusive. Brainstorm as freely as you can. Break loose. Let your mind roam in search of fresh ideas. Your PMMS will work best if you actually write your lists down, using pencil and paper. Just thinking about it won't be effective. Whether you use the worksheets provided in this book or a separate notebook, all the information you collect will be organized and immediately available.

Again, be as complete as you can, and don't be too hard on yourself in your ability ranking. If consummate skill were required to be a success in music, many TV and pop stars would be driving trucks. Does Rod Stewart have a good voice?

Making these lists will be a continuing process, and you will add to or modify them frequently. You will find that having this information in front of you is very useful, and you'll begin to make connections and get jobs that you probably never would have otherwise considered.

Making connections between your talents and the music marketplace is exactly what the Personal Music Marketing System is supposed to do, and these lists will help guide you to new, lucrative uses for your music.

7

Your Job Possibilities List

Now you have a complete assessment of your musical abilities, strengths, and equipment. You know all the musical things you can do, which ones you do best, and which ones need work.

Your next task is to locate as many possible kinds of jobs as you can—jobs that will need, could use, or might possibly benefit from your music. In making this Job Possibilities list, you'll want your creativity to swing into high gear.

Again, the usefulness of the list depends on how complete it is. The more possible job categories you include, the more you'll work and the more money you will make. This Job Possibilities list will come from your experience, imagination, creative brainstorming, and a little market research.

The main idea here is to think of as many different kinds or types of music jobs as you can. Include jobs that you might be only remotely suited for. Don't worry about the practicality of opportunities at this stage.

Don't even think about whether the jobs actually exist!

Especially, don't limit your list to the same old kinds of jobs you've always played. Just list the types and broad categories of musical jobs that interest you and all that you think you could possibly handle.

- *Be creative.*
- *Engage in wishful thinking.*
- *Practice brainstorming.*
- *Spend time associating.*
- *Dream up some fantastic goals.*

You should even try to invent jobs that would use your music. Just because no one is playing such jobs now doesn't mean you can't.

Your task here is to stay out of the ruts into which most musicians fall. There is plenty of work out there. You just have to find it, and the reward is money. It's up to you to discover that work and reap the reward.

Don't say, "I'm a guitarist, so I can only work with top-forty lounge bands." Instead, stretch your idea of what a guitar can do to include other kinds of music. Can you play classical acoustic guitar? Couldn't you play solo jobs? Do you sing? How is your jazz work? Do you know standard tunes? What about playing shows? How's your reading? Have you ever taught? Are you interested in repair work?

Don't say, "I'm a vocalist, so all I can do is sing in a church choir." Think instead of all the places that singing could be used and expand your market thinking to include backup singing in clubs or at concerts, recording-studio work on jingles and demo sessions, singing at weddings, producing your own show (for conventions, trade shows, cruise ships), teaching and coaching, singing in restaurants and lounges, work in dinner theaters, and playing roles in musicals. Can you sing in different styles? Do you like people? Do you enjoy the spotlight and applause? Think big. Dream creatively to expand the possible markets for your music.

When you think like this, you'll come up with other kinds of situations that could use your music. Furthermore, you might even devise jobs that neither the agents in your area nor your potential clients have thought of. Fine! Great! You'll have that new field all to yourself.

REMEMBER THE MUSICAL ELF

One enterprising flutist I know convinced the manager of a large department store to hire her at Christmastime to walk around the store, dressed as an elf, playing Christmas carols. She had devised an unconventional job for herself—and a lucrative one—by thinking creatively. She had invented a job that was hers alone.

As you work on your job possibilities list, don't limit yourself to jobs that you've already played. Invent new ones! Make up a reason to have a party that will feature your music. Suggest celebrations of important—or whimsical—events.

Virtually every day and week of the year is special for some reason, and Appendix E lists lots of reasons, or excuses, for celebration. Maybe it's National Goof-off Day (March 22), National Pasta Week (October 3-12), or National Griper's Day (April 15). Perhaps a local radio station would like to sponsor a Friday-the-thirteenth after-work party featuring your band, or an apartment complex would like to have a midnight celebration of the return of Halley's comet. Why not?

Let your imagination work, put your mind in neutral, and brainstorm to see how many ideas you can come up with. Start with the traditional kinds of jobs that you've played, or thought of playing someday, and go on from there.

NOW FOR THE MENTAL JOGGING

When you are sure that you have thought of every type of job that might possibly need you, there are still two important steps to take. First, you've got to jog your creativity again. Go back to your "kinds of music I can do" list as a stimulant for brainstorming your newly created Job Possibilities list.

Let your mind be imaginative about each item, play association games, and see what you can come up with. Does playing chamber music in a bank lobby make you think of playing chamber music in a shopping mall? Or in a large office-building cafeteria just before Thanksgiving? Good, you're associating and on your way to a longer job-types list.

Second, after you've made your list as complete as possible, read the next three chapters. Don't read them now. Wait until you've expanded your own listing of job categories so that the suggestions in those chapters won't limit your thinking.

The next three chapters list many kinds of jobs for free-lance musicians. Each entry includes short explanatory comments. These ideas are provided only to get you started in expanding and diversifying your own list. Your list should reflect opportunities in your own community, and it may end up being shorter or much longer than the suggestions offered here.

Remember, your Job Possibilities list will be yours alone, and the more creative you can be in discovering kinds of jobs that can use your music, the more you'll be in demand. This list will guide you as you develop your marketing plan, so work to make it as comprehensive as you can.

8

Kinds of Jobs that Need You

Before you read the next four chapters you should have compiled your own Job Possibilities list, and it should be as long as you can make it. I offer many suggestions here, but this isn't a "complete" list of all freelance music job possibilities. Such a list would be impossible to compile since the freelance market is always growing and changing. These job categories cover much of the musical spectrum, and every single one won't apply to you. Some will match your situation; others will stimulate new ideas. You may be able to add entire categories not discussed here. Your final compilation should be relevant to your community needs and your own music.

Some of these jobs will fit your own abilities today. Others may be too difficult, demanding, or involved for you to play right now. If so, put them on your list anyway, as "goals for the future," and work on getting ready to play them. Some of the jobs listed here may require extensive preparation, while others may be very simple for you. Don't expect each category to be equally easy. In fact, the jobs that require the most work may turn out to be the most rewarding.

If you live in a large city or near a resort area, your list of Job Possibilities may eventually grow so long that it overwhelms you, whereas if you live in a smaller community or rural area, you will have slimmer pickings. In either case, you'll be able to find more jobs if you start with an organized and comprehensive summary of the kinds of jobs you can play.

Don't be concerned with practicality at this point. Just keep thinking of *kinds of jobs you might possibly play*. Obviously, the more categories you list for your music, the more jobs you'll find. So keep on adding to your list and thinking up similar applications for your music.

At the risk of repeating myself, I'll say it again: *Write your ideas down*. That way, you'll be building a system, not just a collection of random thoughts. As you compile your basic Job Possibilities list, however, don't be concerned about how to book any particular job. That comes later. In Chapter 12, "Contact People," we'll discuss how to locate the people who need your music.

NIGHTCLUBS

Nightclubs and cabarets offer an abundance of work to the freelance musician. Players who work steadies (five or six nights a week) as well as those who only play one-nighters should keep up with the local musical scene.

There are almost as many kinds of clubs as kinds of popular music: top-forty clubs, oldies clubs, swing-music big-band clubs, country-and-western clubs, show rooms, new-wave clubs, and jazz spots. You'll find tiny bistros with barely room for a solo guitarist on a stool in the corner, clubs that specialize in huge productions of Las Vegas-type revues, and stylish restaurants and lounges that use string quartets. Whatever your specialty, you'll probably find a club that needs it.

If you, or your group, are interested in club work as your musical mainstay, several good books provide guidance toward success in this always competitive market (see Appendix B). The nightclub world is too broad to cover in detail here, but these suggestions will help you succeed.

Decide what kind of club you want to work in and concentrate on producing the appropriate style of music. If you want to get in a motel lounge circuit, for example, find out what type and size band is typically hired, and act accordingly. Should four-piece groups with a female vocalist seem to be the norm, you wouldn't stand much chance with a seven-man band.

Find out what management expects before you take the job, and stay open to suggestion during the engagement. Remember, club owners are interested in filling the room and making money. As elsewhere in the music world, you'll have to produce the kind of music your client thinks will attract customers. Don't expect to play very much original material in a Holiday Inn lounge, or a lot of jazz in a resort show club.

Prepare for very hard work. Steady, every-night club engagements are physically and mentally demanding. Figure out how to stay interested in your music, take an occasional night off, and try not to succumb to boredom. Playing the same music every night for people who are mostly interested in drinking, dancing, or meeting members of the opposite sex can be very frustrating.

Get a written contract. Every musician over the age of twelve has heard horror stories of crooked club owners and shady operators. If you don't get paid on Saturday, don't go to work on Monday. To gain additional clout when negotiating, join a union if one is active in your area.

Consider occasional work. What if you're not interested in steady, every-night club work? You should still stay in touch with club owners and the working club musicians in your area because there are other opportunities for you. A few examples:

• Often clubs will have special events that call for extra musicians or groups—a special show, a Mother's Day brunch, or a New Year's Eve party with a large, out-of-town band.

• Some smaller clubs use music one or two nights a week only and rotate groups regularly. Weekend work might fit your schedule better than trying to play every night.

• Daytime jobs are becoming more common in many areas. Music is provided for luncheons, fashion shows, wedding receptions, and business meetings that are held in club or restaurant facilities.

● Substitute work for steadily employed musicians can offer opportunities if you are available on short notice. When the drummer in a top-forty band is sick, the show must go on regardless, and you could pick up the extra work if he or she knows of your availability.

RESTAURANTS

Restaurants, particularly the finer, more elaborate ones, offer much work for the freelance musician. Here are some typical needs:

Background or dinner music is usually restful, soothing, sophisticated, and elegant. The most frequently needed instruments are piano, organ, accordion, violin, harp, and guitar, but many others can be used. Flute and piano, or cello and piano, or other uncommon combinations—perhaps violin and harpsichord—provide an unusual, pleasant sound that dinner patrons will appreciate. Often, of course, typical dance bands are used.

Don't forget special holidays or particular events. Even restaurants that don't normally use music might be receptive on St. Patrick's Day, during Oktoberfest, or on the restaurant's tenth anniversary. (See Appendix E for more suggestions.)

Ethnic music is appropriate in many restaurants, and this can be quite exotic. If, for example, you play the balalaika, there is probably a Russian restaurant looking for you.

Many smaller cities in the United States are increasingly cosmopolitan, with mixed populations and a growing variety of restaurants—Greek, Indonesian, French, Thai, Middle Eastern, and so on. Each requires related and appropriate music.

Special events. Wedding receptions, club dances, private cocktail parties, retirement or promotion functions, and anniversary celebrations of groups or couples often take place in restaurants. A good relationship with the management can result in many referrals for parties that you otherwise would not know about.

Lunchtime music is becoming common in better restaurants and hotel lounges in many areas. Don't hesitate to suggest this idea to the restaurants in your area, particularly the ones that use music at night or have a substantial lunchtime business.

Many restaurants feature music in the dining room for the early evening and switch to the lounge later on. Don't overlook the possibility of playing both places, particularly if your repertory is broad enough to handle both dinner and dance requirements.

Of course, many restaurants feature the same musicians every night, but there are many occasions for extra or different music—special events, a particular week- or month-long promotion—or the need arises occasionally for substitutes for steadily employed musicians. Stay up-to-date on the restaurant world in your area.

HOTELS

Because of the great number of conventions, business meetings, and social events that take place in hotels, make it a priority to stay in touch with hotel people. Often they will be your best source of leads and will refer clients to you.

Moreover, hotels often have their own musical needs, including:

Music in the lounge. Even the dedicated freelancer may work a steady job, from time to time, or do substitute work for regularly employed musicians.

Music in the lobby. Many larger hotels use soothing and sophisticated music in the lobby or lobby bar. This is particularly true during busy conventions and holiday seasons. Piano or guitar are probably most common, but this is an excellent opportunity for small pop or jazz groups, strings, or even classical players.

Music for hotel-sponsored parties. Hotels sometimes give parties for their regular clients and for their own employees.

SUBSTITUTE WORK

As mentioned already, substitute or fill-in work can be an important area for freelance income. Musicians who work all those steady engagements in nightclubs, restaurants, and lounges get sick as everyone else does, and they need occasional vacations. Enterprising freelance players will stay in touch with musicians who are working steadies and make known their availability.

Many musicians are justifiably afraid of losing their steady jobs; often they are only "two weeks' notice" away from unemployment. If you are interested in doing substitute work, make it clear that you are not after the job permanently and that you will not try to displace the player for whom you are subbing. Other players will be more likely to hire you if they trust you.

One other thing to remember is that per-night pay on a steady engagement is usually less than you make from one-night jobs. You should be willing to sub for whatever the going nightly pay is, and the person hiring you should pay you what he or she would normally make for the time you fill in.

In large cities, subs can work frequently—perhaps as much as they'd like—simply by staying in touch with the six-night musicians in the area. The pay may be relatively low, but the work can be easy and the change stimulating.

SCHOOLS

Schools offer a broad market for all kinds of music. Here are a few of their needs:

Substitute teaching is an excellent opportunity for the free-lancer who holds a teaching certificate. Check with all the school districts in your area, including private and church institutions, for policies and needs. A few days of substitute teaching each month can make a sizable difference in your income, and the daytime work won't interfere with your evening music jobs.

Nursery schools may employ part-time music teachers to lead singing or other music activities. If you enjoy working with children, you could become the visiting teacher at one or more nursery schools. A college degree in music or education would be helpful but is usually not essential. You might even team up with puppeteers, jugglers, clowns, or actors to produce simple shows for nursery and elementary school audiences.

College theatrical or musical groups will frequently need professional soloists or musicians. Watch for announcements, casting calls, and tryouts. Often no pay is offered, but sometimes there will be a budget for adding professionals.

Accompanying for recitals, particularly near colleges or conservatories, can be a good way for pianists to make money. Pianists who are in school themselves can avail themselves of this opportunity if they have the time. Voice and instrumental majors are often required to give recitals, and their accompanists usually are paid.

Concerts for the college student body (often sponsored by the student association or the college's activity fund) usually feature famous entertainers or locally known groups, which frequently need backup musicians. Or, if you have a packaged show that would appeal to college-age audiences, such as a "History of Rock and Roll" show or an outstanding jazz revue, why not try to book your own act? Since many colleges have monthly concerts, this is a continuing market for a wide spectrum of music.

Fraternities and sororities at schools, colleges, and universities are a steady market for rock, pop, soul, and country bands, shows, and soloists. (And don't overlook fraternal organizations at vocational and technical schools.) The so-called Greek organizations are thriving again all across the nation, holding dances and parties as often as deans will allow. Rush week at the beginning of the school year is particularly active.

Also, many Greek organizations—essentially fraternities and sororities—exist independently of the college world. Many of these are professional associations, others are vocation related, and some are entirely social. Most of these clubs hold dances at least annually, and many sponsor social functions throughout the year.

Student parties of every description have always been a staple of college life. Fraternities and sororities use lots of music, of course, but so do other organizations within a school. Party sponsors may include the student center, student activities fund, alumni association, and special-interest groups. College students love dances, parties, reunions, street fairs, and carnivals, and for many students such events are as important as classroom work. You should help students enjoy themselves with your music.

College-sponsored fund-raising and social activities sometimes require music. For example, cocktail parties are typically given for
wealthy alumni and contributors, often before or after athletic events.
Fairs, carnivals, pageants, or dances may be staged to raise money.
Sometimes these events are handled through a school's music department, but not always. Stay in touch through alumni offices, school publications, and public-relations directors.

Class reunions are held by the thousand every year—usually
in May or June—for alumni of high schools, vo-tech schools, and colleges. Almost all of these functions need music, especially music related
to the class graduation year.
   This area has an especially appealing side for many musicians.
No matter what your age—and to some extent that determines your musical priorities—there are class reunions from your era that need your
kind of music. If your heart is in big-band music because you went to
school in the forties, you can be sure that, somewhere, the class of 1948
wants you. Or if you remember all the Beatles tunes because that's when
you were in college, you'll probably find that the class of 1970 remem-
bers those songs, too, and will enjoy reminiscing with you.
   If your repertory includes songs from a particular year or era—or
if you can present an after-dinner musical revue of the hits of that year—
these parties could be very lucrative for you and your group. Be prepared
to provide music for skits and other staged events as well as for the dinner
and the dance.

Grants or other special funds are available for presenting
educational programs in schools. The Music Performance Trust Fund
(MPTF) of the American Federation of Musicians is an example of a program that promotes various live music productions, often in the schools.
   Often the pay for these programs is low, since the event is educational, but it's usually daytime work and good public relations for you. If
you diligently pursue performance grants, you can even specialize, like
the two brothers from Maryland who make their living traveling the eastern United States, presenting educational jazz concerts and workshops at
small colleges and universities.
   Government and foundation sources also can fund this kind of
activity. If your talents and interests are in the educational performance
area, your librarian can direct you to some excellent books on grants-
manship (see Appendix B), and the musicians union can give you details
on the MPTF program.

WEDDINGS

Marriage ceremonies require many types of music and can be a steady source of income to freelance musicians. People will get married even in bad economic times, and families usually want music for such important occasions. The use of music is not limited to wealthy families or to traditional indoor church weddings. All marriage ceremonies can benefit from good music.

Since weddings are once-in-a-lifetime events (in theory at least), it's not unusual for families to spend more lavishly than might be expected. *Bride's Magazine* reports that, in 1983, the average wedding cost $4,376, with liquor at the reception accounting for $432 and flowers costing $268. The music should be an essential part of the plan; remind the families involved that the entertainment cost will be only a fraction of their total expenditures.

Organists or pianists most commonly play for the ceremony itself, but almost any other pleasing instrument or combination can be used. What if you aren't a pianist or organist? Since brides and bridal consultants are often open to innovative ideas, suggest different possibilities, depending on your instrument. Tell your prospects what you can do with harp, flute, classical guitar, woodwind quintet, or string quartet. Less common instruments, such as harpsichord or lute, can be very appropriate, and the unique sound will please the bridal party and the wedding guests. Use your imagination in this category, and you'll see your job market expand.

Rehearsal dinners and receptions also need music. The rehearsal dinner will probably be more lively than the reception following the marriage ceremony and will likely need a more contemporary band. Reception music can range from strictly background music—solo piano, harp, or strolling violin, for example—to a large dance orchestra.

Wealthy families are often interested in bringing in an out-of-town or even a "name" band, so cities and towns within driving distance of your home might be excellent markets.

Brides and their families want their weddings to be memorable and happy occasions, and the enterprising musicians who can make practical suggestions regarding instrumentation and repertory will often be able to create more work for themselves.

Remember that although you, the musician, may be the music expert, you should become familiar with what type of music the bride prefers. By anticipating and filling her musical needs, you can make yourself invaluable.

BAR MITZVAHS

Bar mitzvahs and bas mitzvahs are, like weddings, family affairs. The mood is often celebratory, and the family and guests are intent on having a good time. In some places, these events are rather rigidly styled and follow a strict pattern. In other communities, a bar mitzvah may be more like a large family party with a few horas thrown in.

The musician who is familiar with Jewish music and tradition will find a large market here, and, as with weddings, word-of-mouth advertising will lead to many unsolicited jobs. As with weddings, Jewish families will have these celebrations in good times and bad, and they offer a continuing market for freelance musicians.

Frequently there will be a reception before the dinner-dance that will call for background music, affording a good opportunity for harpists, accordionists, acoustic guitarists, pianists, or small groups of almost any sort. Such occasions can be particularly lucrative to the musician who is versatile enough to play both segments—a guitarist, for example, who can play classical music during the reception and with the dance band afterwards.

Often it is up to the musician who is booking the job to think of these matters and make suggestions to the client. The father may never have thought of using a harp during the reception, but if you mention it, he may love the idea. Or you might suggest a theme party to the family; perhaps an idea based on the son or daughter's interests would be appropriate. As with all potential jobs you pursue, be creative with your suggestions, and you will open many doors for your music.

You'll also find that one good job will lead to another—perhaps to several others. Word-of-mouth advertising is the best kind, and one good bar mitzvah or wedding can do more to spread your name around town than several sales calls.

COUNTRY—AND OTHER—CLUBS

Clubs of all sorts—their variety is astounding—need lots of music for many occasions.

The most obvious clients are country and athletic clubs with their imposing buildings and beautiful golf courses. These clubs have well-defined and regular needs for music and should be kept aware of what you have to offer. Here are typical country club events that all freelancers should remember.

Regularly scheduled dances for club members, often on Friday and Saturday nights, sometimes use the same bands on a rotating schedule. Musicians in these bands must know the characteristics of the membership and be able to play their particular requests.

Special dances, such as on Valentine's Day or New Year's Eve, may require larger dance bands than usual. See if you or your group could be used in such a special band. There's no reason your quartet couldn't add a few pieces when a larger band is needed. Such events are planned months in advance.

Seasonal and holiday activities, sponsored by the club itself, may be as varied as the social director's (and your) imagination will allow. Typical functions include summertime pool parties, Labor Day cookouts, Oktoberfests, Halloween parties for members' children, Christmas and New Year's events, Mother's and Father's Day dances, and many others. Your suggestions—especially if they tie in with a particular event—will be welcomed. (See Appendix E for a list of holidays and annual events.)

Athletic events, such as golf and tennis tournaments, will often begin or end with dances and parties. Keep up with each club's major athletic events by reading its newsletter. If your music is easily mobile, you might suggest a party on the tennis courts or at the eighteenth hole after a tournament.

Shows are often presented for the entertainment of club members. Sometimes a name act will bring its own backup group, but often these performers will rely on local musicians. If you can play shows, be sure that the leaders and contractors in your area keep you in mind. And leaders and contractors, especially, should stay in touch with larger clubs.

Theme parties can be elaborate, and musical requirements may be quite specific. Perhaps the club's members will be involved in a fifties dance, or a roaring-twenties extravaganza, or a Hawaiian/tropical-theme pool party. If your specialty is ethnic, geographic, or unusual music, be sure that the club's social committee knows what you can offer. Theme parties are discussed in more detail in the next chapter.

If you help the social director come up with an unusual idea to beat the boring same-old-party syndrome, you'll be an instant favorite. Always keep thinking and making suggestions.

Children's parties are another country club market. If you can team up with a magician, juggler, mime, puppet show, or similar act, many clubs will welcome you—and pay well for your services. Again, remember that the social committee may be looking desperately for some activity to involve young people. Your suggestions can generate jobs.

Special events, which are essentially private parties given by club members for their guests, may be held in, and booked through, the club. Wedding receptions, office parties, retirement dinners, class reunions, and many other such events may be held in a club's facilities. Music needs will vary, so stay in touch.

Other clubs may not have their own facilities, but they may still be excellent markets for your music. Groups of joggers, marathon runners, softball players, Frisbee devotees—any group that is organized for a specific purpose may have at least one social event each year that uses music. For example, the Atlanta Ski Club holds dances almost monthly. It is one of the largest social clubs in the city even though it rarely snows in Atlanta. Don't limit your job ideas to the obvious ones.

Another source for freelance music leads is the almost endless variety of organized hobby groups—philatelists, photography buffs, model railroad clubs, amateur radio operators, tall-peoples' clubs, short-peoples' clubs, antique car restorers, square dancers, experimental aircraft builders. Almost all such groups will have dances, banquets, cocktail parties, barbecues, picnics, or other regular social events. They need your music.

Thus, as you compile your list, define "clubs" as broadly as you can, but don't limit yourself just to large, established country clubs. By including every organized group you can think of, you will expand the market for your music.

PARTIES IN HOMES

Parties in homes are another special, but excellent, market. Most home parties employing musicians are given by well-to-do people. It is important, therefore, to be able to relate socially as well as musically. Perhaps an elegant dinner party will require sophisticated piano background, or a wedding reception will need a string quartet, or a garden party will need a dance band.

Personal interaction is what these parties are about, and you should be able to talk comfortably with the hosts and guests. In fact, the better you fit in, the better you'll do at these affairs. Therefore you should take pains to look your best—and display your best party behavior.

The nonmusical aspects of these small parties are especially important. Since you are in someone else's home, you have to be careful. Don't be like the drummer who tracked motor oil from his leaking van onto the client's priceless Oriental rug. Don't emulate the guitarist who carelessly turned around and broke an heirloom vase with the neck of his guitar. Nor do you want to repeat the performance of the pianist who set off the host's burglar alarm by moving the grand piano a few inches—without realizing that under-the-carpet sensors were connected to the local police station.

It's easy to scratch floors, mar walls, spill drinks, and generally make yourself unwelcome. With a little care, however, you'll avoid such pitfalls and help make the event a success. And when *you're* the one who makes the party click, you'll become a regular fixture at these soirees.

People at parties often like to stand around the piano and sing. This is good for you if you are a pianist, your repertory is extensive, and you get along well with people. The word will spread, and you will be in demand.

You may be able to "train" the wealthy party givers in your area to expect your music at all the "best" parties, and in doing this you may create not just a few jobs but a whole career.

If you remember names, faces, and favorite tunes of your clients and their friends, they'll think you're terrific (sometimes regardless of your musical skills), and they'll want you at all their parties. (See Appendix B for books to improve your memory.)

9

More Jobs

PUBLIC RELATIONS AND ADVERTISING

Public-relations firms and advertising agencies can be good music clients because they are involved in creating and staging all kinds of events. Whatever your musical specialty, you should let all the PR firms in your area know, so that when they have a need for your type of music, they'll know whom to call.

Many of the jobs included here, and most of those in this chapter, will frequently be booked through PR or entertainment agencies. They are discussed here so you'll have a complete idea of what's involved. Whether a job is booked through an agent or directly by the musician, of course, doesn't alter what the client needs, or what the musicians are expected to perform. Here are some examples.

Political campaign appearances, fund raisers, and victory celebrations are enlivened by dixieland, country, or rock bands. Such events are often planned by the advertising or PR firm that is handling the politician's campaign.

Ground-breaking ceremonies for new buildings of every sort can use music to help create the appropriate mood, which might be exciting and casual, or sophisticated. For example, a large bank in Atlanta recently hired (through its PR agency) a string quartet to play for a black-tie cocktail party at the ground-breaking festivities at the site of a new headquarters—in the middle of a suburban woods.

New product introductions can be produced with true show-business extravagance. Trumpeters with herald trumpets, for example, lend a special air to such events with colorful costumes, banners, and fanfares. A car show might feature a country band for the new truck display, and a sophisticated jazz quartet for the introduction of a new line of luxury passenger cars.

Grand openings for all kinds of new buildings are often celebrated with lavish parties. Whether it's a skyscraper, parking garage, or airplane hangar, the developer's PR firm will handle the party plans, including music.

Office parties are important business functions for many professionals. Stockbrokers, attorneys, accountants, and many others need a chance to socialize with current and potential clients. Their parties can be lavishly produced and often enlivened with music. Again, PR firms may hire the musicians, typically a single performer or small combo.

These events, and many more, have one thing in common: They are arranged by public-relations and advertising firms to draw attention to their client's events or products. If your music can serve such a commercial purpose, public-relations people will love you.

Public-relations firms and advertising agencies thrive on creativity and often are open to suggestions for new or unusual uses of music. When you talk with PR or advertising firms, then, be as creative as you can. Make suggestions that are too innovative to present to other clients. You will be treated as a kindred spirit.

CONVENTIONS AND MEETINGS

The convention and meetings market is one of the fastest-growing areas in contemporary American business. Almost every fair-sized city wants to be a convention center, and every large hotel or resort has a sales staff searching for organizations to hold meetings of all sorts. Virtually every business, industry, government agency, social group, and professional association (and there are thousands of them) has, at the least, an annual meeting or convention to discuss common interests and plan for the coming year.

This market offers an enormous opportunity to musicians, and many freelancers in major convention cities make a comfortable living from the convention trade. If you are aware of what the convention industry needs, you can take steps to make your musical abilities known.

Musical needs of the convention industry cover the spectrum from solo background performers to thirty-piece orchestras backing the biggest names in entertainment. Convention planners often try to give their members and guests the time of their lives, and money may be no object. It is not uncommon for a major convention to spend more than $50,000 on a single evening's show, and the total entertainment budget may be several times that. Music may be needed from breakfast to late night, after-hours events.

Every convention is different, of course. The three hundred members of your state's Water Pollution Engineers Association may have little in common with the American Medical Association, but both groups will probably need a variety of music.

Here are some of the musical needs that a typical convention might have:

Breakfasts use music to wake up the troops or to set a mood, particularly if a specific theme is important to the meeting. The music is often bright and cheerful—a good possibility for banjos and dixieland combos. Early-morning music may also call for single performers or jazz trios.

If you live in an area associated with a certain type of music, then that specialty could be appropriate. Thus, country music would be big in Nashville, western music is popular in Dallas, and dixieland sets the mood in New Orleans. Most convention planners like geographic specialties, whether in food or entertainment, so play this aspect of your location for as much as you can.

Daytime meetings need music for several reasons. Marches and other exciting tunes establish an upbeat tone, particularly if you are playing for a sales-oriented meeting. Walk-up music and fanfares are needed for awards. There may be company skits or even elaborate shows that require full orchestras.

Frequently, new products are introduced to the sales staff at conventions, and these events may be major multimedia productions in which music plays a central part. Contractors and leaders should be prepared for this kind of work.

A small strolling group, perhaps dixieland again, is often used to announce that meetings are about to begin and will play walk-in music for those in attendance.

Lunches need background music, of course, and again it may be related to the convention's theme. If the meeting is composed mostly of men, a female performer may be welcome, whereas a male may be preferred for a women's group. (This may appear discriminatory, but you'll often find it to be the case, and you should prepare sales presentations with this aspect of the business in mind.)

Because conventioneers usually talk business during lunch, subdued music is often desired. Luncheons offer a good opportunity for the unusual instrument or group, so music that is not appropriate for dancing will often be chosen for lunchtime music.

Special events may be held for the families of those attending large conventions, and they'll present musical opportunities. Strolling musicians may work on tour buses or at local attractions visited by the conventioneers. Or musical programs and variety shows may provide the entertainment for a spouses' luncheon. There may be an impromptu talent show by the members themselves—or a magic or puppet show for their children. Fashion shows are common and also need music.

Convention planners often wonder what to do with, and for, the spouses and children of conventioneers. If you make specific suggestions involving your musical talents, you may increase your bank balance considerably.

Cocktail parties and hospitality suites are mainstays of the convention industry. Often, the real business of the convention—the wheeling and dealing—will take place in the informal atmosphere of a hospitality suite. Frequently your client will not be the convention itself but a related business or association.

Thus, at a bankers convention there will be several hospitality suites sponsored by large banks and the companies that serve them—perhaps computer firms, software providers, office-furnishings dealers, and large printing outfits. Many of these companies will spend enormous amounts of money to please and impress their clients, and the freelance musician can often be an important part of the hospitality suite's success.

Musical needs of hospitality suites can cover the musical spectrum. Often a single piano, accordion, violin, or guitar may be appropriate, but just as frequently a small combo that can start the evening with background music and gradually shift to dance music will be wanted.

Sometimes sing-along piano will be just right to attract people to the suite and to encourage conviviality. Perhaps there is a company or convention theme, or maybe a particular kind of music will be suggested by the season—Irish tunes in March, for example, or Christmas songs in December.

The hosts, in cocktail party or hospitality settings, are anxious to impress their clients, and musicians can help by making creative suggestions. If you can consistently provide the kind of music that's needed, you can become an invaluable resource to the meeting planners in your area.

Whatever your musical specialty, there is probably a need for it somewhere in a convention hospitality suite!

Convention dinners can be elaborate and will often need background or dance music. As discussed above, the music may be linked to the convention's theme. Perhaps the band will need to play national anthems or state songs to salute those in attendance. Perhaps a baroque ensemble will be needed or a barbershop quartet to serenade the attendees. Maybe the convention planners would like bluegrass music, or a performance by the local symphony orchestra, or the high school jazz band. Anything goes.

Dances are held in conjunction with many conventions. They offer to those attending a chance to relax and socialize—and talk a little business at the same time. Three factors influence the kind of music that will be required.

First, the conventioneers will want to talk. That's why they're together in the first place. So the music can't be too loud. Second, the crowd will probably be quite mixed in ages and backgrounds, so a variety of music will be needed. Finally, for some reason, people like to hear songs that remind them of home, even if they've only been gone for a day or two. Be prepared, then, to do more geographic area songs than usual—"San Francisco," "Indiana," "Carolina Moon," "New York, New York," and so on. It's a good idea to keep a list of such tunes lest you be stumped by a persistent conventioneer from South Dakota.

Shows are usually the main entertainment focus of the convention, and they can be elaborate. If you are a contractor or bandleader, you may be called on to back the show. Be sure you are capable, both musically and technically, but don't overlook this potentially lucrative part of convention life.

Since entertainment budgets are frequently huge and audiences affluent and sophisticated, it's not uncommon for conventions to stage Las Vegas-style, high-quality shows. At large conventions, such shows—particularly when much money is involved—will usually be booked by an entertainment agency. Even if you don't book the job, however, you can still profit from it. No matter what instrument you play, be sure that all the agencies, leaders, and contractors in your area know about your show-playing ability.

If you become part of a self-contained show, you may be able to sing, play, and dance your way into a full-time career of convention entertaining. Such groups as The Spurlows, The Young Americans, and The Arbors command hefty fees and stay busy on the convention circuit, but they aren't widely known outside this growing and specialized area.

Or, if you are a strong solo performer, talented, and personable, and you have good stage presence, charisma, and lots of ambition, you may want to work toward becoming a convention entertainer in your own right. Such performers as Skip DeVol, Brenda Byers, and Danny Gans entertain at conventions around the world and are constantly in demand.

Theme parties at conventions may be elaborate and require specific kinds of music. By staying in touch with hotels and convention planners in your area, you'll be aware of the types of parties that are frequently given. Common ones are Hawaiian, shipwreck, M*A*S*H*, disco, country/western, fifties, roaring twenties, and many others.

If you play in a steel band, say, you may not work every wedding reception that comes along, but your availability might make an "islander" theme party possible. And if the convention planners know of your availability, they may even plan entire parties around your music.

Whatever your specialty—whether it's fifties rock and roll, or forties swing music, or Gay Nineties sing-along and honky-tonk songs—be sure to let the party planners know so that your music can be a central part of their events.

Convention work covers a broad spectrum and includes virtually any kind of music. The convention planners who put these meeting together, and the booking agents who work with them, are looking for entertainment—sometimes desperately. If your suggestions, backed by a good reputation and professional appearance, can help them avoid the "same old thing," you'll be appreciated and in demand.

SALES MEETINGS

Sales meetings are similar to conventions but are usually smaller and are produced by individual companies. Music is often used to motivate employees and excite others in the audience about the company's plans and products. Music can be required for skits (which probably will need rehearsals), sales awards, sports awards, and many walk-ons and walk-offs. Sometimes there are company songs, and these can be taken very seriously by the company, though their musical value may be questionable.

In sales meeting situations, you need to realize that music, while important, plays a secondary role. The upbeat atmosphere is what is crucial, and there may be little or no room for musical subtlety. If you are offended by loud music and cheerleader-type repetition, sales meetings may not be for you. On the other hand, these events aren't too demanding, and they offer daytime income, a plus for most freelance musicians.

Frequently, a company will be giving away a trip as a sales incentive, and the music will be thematically related to an exotic destination—maybe Hawaii, Spain, or the Bahamas. Get this information in advance and be prepared with the appropriate instrumentation and repertory—maybe even specially rented costumes.

BUSINESSES

Businesses of all kinds are good possibilities for a great variety of music. Large companies, department stores, or professional firms will be good prospects, but don't overlook smaller concerns.

Each business-related musical need may apply to dozens—or hundreds—of different companies. It's up to you to relate your ideas and your kind of music to department stores, insurance agencies, car dealers, manufacturing plants, law firms, and so on. Tracking down all the music opportunities in the business world could be a full-time job.

Often these events will be produced by advertising, public-relations, or entertainment agencies. Larger companies particularly will leave the details to such outside party planners, as discussed at the beginning of this chapter, and you'll need to stay in touch with the agencies in your area to book these jobs. Other companies, however, prefer to plan and put on such functions themselves, so don't overlook the possibility of booking these jobs directly when you make your marketing plans.

Here are several types of business events that may need your music services:

Ground-breaking ceremonies for new buildings are big events, and related music helps make the occasion really special. The music usually reflects the building's theme or purpose—or adds excitement. A country band, then, might be appropriate for a new truck dealership, while a strolling violin duo could create the right atmosphere for a new, exclusive jewelry store's opening festivities. Or a top-forty band could play for the younger sales force of a real estate developer when a major subdivision is begun. You may have to rent a portable generator if the location is remote.

Grand openings of anything from factories to department stores can be celebrated with upbeat, inspiring, exciting music.

Seasonal sales can feature anything appropriate—for example, a brass band at a car dealer's for September's introductory sales, or an elegant flute and harpsichord duo in a fur salon for the fall specials. One large store uses Mexican-style bands to introduce its Holiday Vacation Fiesta, a joint project of the travel, clothing, and camera departments. Your creative suggestions in this area could get you the job.

Trade shows, where businesspeople meet to sell products and swap ideas, frequently use different kinds of music. Trade shows are like conventions but concentrate on displays and products instead of meetings. Your job may be to attract people to a particular booth or display. New-product introductions, particularly, need exciting music.

Promotions and retirements are often celebrated with elaborate parties. Legal, medical, and accounting firms will relax a bit on these occasions and use background or dance music—maybe even in the office. Retirement parties, obviously, should feature the guest of honor's favorite songs; tunes from his or her early years with the company will be appreciated.

Company milestones such as anniversaries, corporate acquisitions, or new construction need to be celebrated and will often need music of some kind.

Christmas parties offer many opportunities. Almost every company has at least one Christmas party. Large concerns may have several: one for the executives, another for the professional staff, and a third for the lower-level employees. Start planning early for the busy December season.

Fashion shows are given by department stores, boutiques, merchandise marts, restaurants, trade associations, country clubs, and civic groups. They may be held in hotel ballrooms, country clubs, theaters, restaurants, or schools. Music is a crucial element, yet sponsors often rely on taped music that is inflexible and frequently of very poor quality. You should sell the show organizers on using you or your group because of the added flexibility and the excitement of live music.

Music requirements will vary according to the nature of the audience, the clothes being shown, and the desires of the director. Some fashion shows will be composed of little more than a few models wearing new clothes and walking through the lunchtime crowd at a fashionable restaurant. Others will be elaborate productions, carefully scripted and planned, and bordering on the complexity of a stage show. Such events will require rehearsal and careful coordination of the music with the clothes being shown; the musician's job is to create a stimulating and appropriate atmosphere.

Part of your task at a fashion show may be that of a translator. You will be asked to provide music to match the clothes or to create a certain mood, and you will probably have to translate such terms as "sophisticated," "bouncy," "urbane," "chic," or even "new" into music. It will help if your repertoire is broad and you don't have to rely on reading all the music you play. Speed and flexibility are important.

SHOPPING MALLS

Huge shopping malls exist in most American cities, and many of them are like towns in themselves. Many people never go downtown anymore, and the local mall, with its theaters, restaurants, and boutiques, is often the real focus of a community's life.

Events sponsored by the mall itself to celebrate a seasonal event use music to attract people and hold crowds. Choral concerts at Christmas, band concerts for the Fourth of July, and German oompah bands for Oktoberfest are examples.

Special sales sponsored by individual stores also use musicians, ranging from a harpist in an elegant fur salon to a country band at the western-wear outlet store. In some areas it is common for car dealers to erect huge tents in a mall's parking lot and stage elaborate "salathons" that use exciting music to attract car buyers.

Larger malls often run weeklong festivals that attract huge crowds, and music is important to these events. Heritage Week or Local Artists Week celebrations need appropriate music—not to mention National Polka Week.

The mall's publicity director will be receptive to ideas that will generate excitement and crowds. Use Appendix E and your creativity to make unique suggestions—with local emphasis, if possible. Maybe the mall could sponsor a jazz festival or even a local composers' concert series. Or you could tie your ideas to traditional sales weeks and have a September back-to-school dance in the mall—or a beach music concert in May or June.

Perhaps your suggestions could be for regular, ongoing events—a tea dance on Friday afternoons or a Sunday morning dixieland brunch. Or you could suggest single acts to circulate throughout the mall entertaining the shoppers. The spontaneity of such "street musicians" would add zest and life to the mall's crowds.

ASSOCIATIONS

In today's information-based business and professional world, people with similar interests are increasingly joining together in associations to share knowledge and data—and to socialize. Many people get an important sense of belonging from membership in an association, and sometimes it's hard to separate the social aspects of associations from their professional and business purposes.

You might be astounded at the number and variety of associations. How many are there? The multivolume *Encyclopedia of Associations* has almost 20,000 entries, including 189 music-related groups. For another example, the 1985 San Francisco telephone book lists more than 400 associations.

Associations represent everybody from red-headed people to makers of liquid fertilizer, from doctors of neurology to Trivial Pursuit players, and from Renaissance music fanatics to college reading teachers. You will be encouraged upon learning how many of these groups are active in your community (the Yellow Pages will get you started in your search) and how many of them use music at their functions.

Associations hold state, regional, and national meetings or conventions. You should certainly become aware of the enormous number and variety of associations that are active in your area, because many of them will have dinners, programs, fund-raisers, and dances that need music, not to mention those annual conventions.

Large associations often book large dance bands or even complete after-dinner shows, while smaller groups use combos or single musicians. Perhaps the members will have a talent show or other activity that you could play for, or perhaps they'd like to feature *you* as the evening's entertainment.

CIVIC, SOCIAL, AND NONPROFIT ORGANIZATIONS

After-dinner shows, dances, and fund-raising events are frequently put on by civic associations and social organizations and they need music. Some, such as the American Legion and the Elks and Moose clubs, have their own facilities, with regularly scheduled dances and social functions. Others, like the Lions and Rotary clubs, will have infrequent social events. The freelance musician should stay in touch with all such organizations and be aware of their changing musical needs.

Often the social or entertainment committee changes each year, and the new officers may have no idea of whom to call to book a band or after-dinner show. They will appreciate learning what you have to offer.

Fund-raising events can be elaborate. Such organizations as hospital auxiliaries, women's clubs, and the Junior League may put on extravagant shows complete with large orchestra, many rehearsals, expensive costumes, and so on—all to raise money for the group's projects. (There is at least one large national company that provides directors, costumes, and music for these organizations to help produce professional-looking shows.)

Since the fund-raising market is a large one, the musician should be aware of all nearby nonprofit organizations. Don't forget civic orchestras, historical preservation societies, opera companies, theaters, health organizations, specific disease-related foundations, and even college athletic associations—all of which may sponsor dinners, dances, or shows to benefit a cause.

Parades, fairs, carnivals, street dances, and many other events are also used to raise money or get publicity. Know which civic association sponsors them.

You may be asked to donate your services, and if you do you can often take a tax deduction for the value of your contribution. But many fund-raising organizations will pay for your musical services, just as they pay for the food they serve, and raise the money from the public. A few benefit gigs may be helpful as advertising, but many might be financially counterproductive.

GOVERNMENT-SPONSORED WORK

You pay taxes, so why not try to get some of that money back by working for your city, state, or federal government? Although governments aren't usually thought of as buyers of music, you may be surprised at the variety of jobs you can find through the bureaucracy. Here are a few examples:

Park programs abound, and governmental or quasi-governmental agencies are often in control. In Atlanta, for example, a Cultural Affairs Bureau sponsors large and small music festivals around the city, and there is even a "Jazzmobile" that goes from park to park during the summer. Usually, local talent is used.

Inner-city festivals, grand openings of newly renovated areas, and parties to celebrate special days are commonly produced by governing boards. When it's your town's centennial or bicentennial, why not suggest a concert in the park or a street dance? The city council or board of aldermen may conduct the affair directly or work with a private-sector sponsor.

Cultural enrichment programs and historical musical services are widespread, and government-sponsored music at national parks and historic sites offers interesting opportunities. If you perform Native American or early American music, you may find a government-owned place to perform. (Don't overlook foundation-sponsored historical centers, such as Old Salem, Williamsburg, and Sturbridge Village.)

Foreign tours to entertain our troops overseas provide work for musicians, entertainers, and groups. Many musicians have spent enjoyable (though hardworking) summers doing USO tours of European, Asian, and other military bases. Navy pilots and other personnel stationed in Greenland need entertainment too.

Each branch of the armed forces has its own bands, and these offer secure employment, travel, and excellent musical experiences for musicians who are interested in full-time playing jobs. Many of these bands are of excellent quality, and they offer stage, jazz, and dance work in addition to traditional ceremonial playing. Often, too, armed-forces band members can accept outside freelance work to augment their incomes.

Officers' clubs, and NCO clubs on most military bases need bands for regularly scheduled dances and for special occasions. Sometimes units from the base's band supply music, but usually outside groups are hired. If you live near a large military installation, it could provide you with a substantial amount of work.

Grants, scholarships, internships, stipends, and student loans are offered by governmental agencies as well as by private foundations or organizations. Each grant or scholarship will have specific requirements and be for a specific purpose, but if you have a musically worthwhile project that needs funding, you should research such sources of money. (See Appendix B for further reading.) Some states offer college scholarships to students who promise to teach school in the state for a specified time, and there are many other sources of government-sponsored education money and student loans.

10

Still More Jobs

THEATERS AND SHOWS

Theaters, both amateur and professional, need music. Musicals must have accompaniment, from rehearsal pianists to pit orchestras. If you are an instrumentalist and a good reader, then playing shows as they come through your area may provide a considerable portion of your freelance income.

If you are a singer, you should be aware of the chorus or backup vocal needs of all the shows that come to town. This includes theatrical productions, concerts, and nightclub acts.

In many places, several theater companies aspire to professional status but constantly battle to survive. These community, semiprofessional theaters may not offer much money, but there should be some compensation. This is an excellent way to get experience and meet people in your field.

Shows featuring famous entertainers pick up local musicians for the orchestra. Well-known acts often will travel with a conductor and pianist and hire all other players locally. Since the theater season can last several months, this can be an especially lucrative market for those players who enjoy it.

Dinner theaters—although an endangered species—offer work to both instrumentalists and singers, including small backup bands. If you are just starting your career, you may find such a theater provides excellent training. If you are an established singer, you may land a lead role. At dinner theaters, where actors and actresses may also wait on tables, the work is hard, but the experience may be rewarding.

Your own show. If you are an entertainer as well as a musician, you may want to produce a show and book it to civic groups, conventions, fairs, festivals, and even cruise ships. To be effective, a show must be well conceived, well written, professionally produced, and—above all—entertaining. Elaborate and expensive productions on television have set the standard for today's audiences. If your singing, jokes, choreography, costumes and—most important—charisma and stage presence don't measure up, you'll find it difficult to succeed.

Since audiences expect a high level of entertainment, you'll have to work hard to put together a successful show. If you do, however, you'll have a very salable product that can be booked "as is" for years. Many successful performers for convention shows—singers, comics, instrumentalists—develop a format that works well and rarely change it.

The market for shows is huge and expanding. Once you've created a successful show, however, your work isn't over. You have to maintain your product. What happens if the featured vocalist gets pregnant? Or goes back to school? Or your guitarist wants to produce his own show? No one ever said that show business would be easy, but if entertaining is in your blood, give it a try.

Entertainment, fast paced and energetic, is what show business is all about. Few instrumentalists can carry an entire show; usually a singer or vocal group is the main attraction. Some solo acts, of course, are very popular and well known to the general public. But dozens of lesser-known groups travel the country performing at conventions and fairs.

Many are very successful, though not widely acclaimed. Such groups as The Arbors, The Spurlows, Main Street, and Showboat have created well-paying careers, and are flourishing in a very competitive area of show business.

CIRCUS, TRAVELING SHOWS, AND SPORTS MUSIC

Circus playing is similar to playing shows, but it is much harder work and happens only once or twice a year. Horn players particularly should stay in touch with local contractors and band leaders to be in line for this work.

Other road shows—ice shows, rodeos, and so on—will use local musicians. These shows will visit all medium-sized and large cities and can provide a week of well-paying work for those who are able to read the charts—and endure the physical demands of nonstop playing.

Ball parks and sports stadiums also need music, and not just an organist for baseball games, either. Pep bands, halftime entertainment, and other excitement-producing music go well with professional sports. This potential market for your music should be explored at local, minor league, and college levels as well as at big league parks.

Note that in July 1983 the Eastman School of Music conducted a sports organist seminar, and this specialized area of musical enterprise was covered in a *Newsweek* story (August 1, 1983).

TOURIST-RELATED JOBS

Tourist-related work may be plentiful and lucrative in your area, but you may need to use your imagination to find—or create—it. Obvious employers include large theme parks such as Six Flags, Disney World, and Carowinds, which use lots of music, but there are others.

Riverboats evoke another era. Every riverboat needs at least a banjo, perhaps a dixieland band.

Historical sites suggest many musical applications. Investigate the state or national parks and battlefields in your area. Such historic restorations as Williamsburg, Old Salem, Sturbridge Village, and West-ville could prove opportune. You might double your chances if you also make, for example, lutes or recorders. By combining this craft with the appropriate music, you could make yourself a featured part of the tourist attraction.

Sightseeing tours sponsored by local companies for conven-tioneers or other touring groups may need special music at various desti-nations or even on the tour bus, boat or train itself.

Cruise ships take thousands of tourists yearly on elaborate va-cation jaunts and use dance bands, show groups, and single performers to provide entertainment for their guests. Headline acts may be well-known performers, but there are numerous opportunities for versatile backup musicians. Sometimes there are special cruises for classical-music lovers, featuring chamber music, small orchestras, and famous soloists.

A restored opera house or theater in your area may provide another opportunity. Visiting groups would enjoy a short show featuring music of the building's original era.

Seasonal festivals or neighborhood celebrations attract many visitors and need a variety of music. Why couldn't your chamber music group work with the botanical gardens activities committee to co-sponsor a concert in the gardens? Or a recital in a restored mansion dur-ing the candlelight tour of homes?

A famous composer or performer from your community need not be alive to help you. A program of his or her music might be just the thing to perform at the birthplace or memorial center—or as an after-dinner show for civic or convention groups.

Hal Holbrook's *Mark Twain Tonight!* is an excellent example of applied creative thinking. Holbrook combined his knowledge of Mark Twain with his acting ability and business sense to create a successful show-business career. Is there something similar you could do that would involve your music?

The possibilities for tourist-related music are almost endless. If you match your imagination and musical ability with some creative mar-keting, you may find jobs where none had existed before.

ORCHESTRAS

Orchestras frequently use supplementary musicians for special concerts, adding extras as the music demands. Good freelance players with appropriate backgrounds should be alert to this possible source of employment.

Classical players can often work with community and professional orchestras in smaller cities or on college campuses. Often such symphony orchestras or chamber groups will draw first-chair players and soloists from larger cities for concerts. So expand your job-search area to include smaller cities and towns within driving distance.

Classical players in Atlanta, for instance, often play with smaller symphony orchestras in cities within a 250-mile radius—Chattanooga, Birmingham, Columbus, Macon, Greenville, Augusta, and Savannah. The market for their music is thus expanded from one to eight cities.

Every large city helps support the arts in smaller surrounding communities this way, and the willingness to make a few hours' drive can improve your market outlook.

CHURCHES AND SYNAGOGUES

Churches and synagogues offer several employment opportunities to a wide variety of musicians. Here are a few possibilities:

Church choirs—especially the larger ones in large cities—may pay their soloists or even their members for performing at regular weekly services. Frequently freelance help is used for special holiday programs or concerts.

Instructors and conductors are needed for orchestra and band activities at an increasing number of churches and synagogues. Some institutions offer opportunities for private or class instruction in voice, instrument, piano, and organ.

Weddings and funerals need music. Sometimes music for these occasions is taken care of by staff musicians, but often outside freelancers are hired. Remember, too, that traditional weddings can involve much more than organ and piano, and that contemporary services can use virtually any kind of music that appeals to the bride and groom. (At one recent wedding in Atlanta, a solo string bass provided the only music—nontraditional but effective.)

Substitute organists, pianists, and choral directors may be needed by churches or synagogues on short notice. Religious services must go on even when the regular organist or choir director is sick or on vacation. If you are available and competent to do fill-in work, let it be known.

Holiday programs often provide a yearly busy season for both vocalists and instrumentalists. One freelance bassist we know regularly plays five or six performances of *The Messiah* during the Christmas season—all paid, of course, and all with paid rehearsals.

The freelance player must be aware of these opportunities and be prepared to do an excellent job with little rehearsal. Even churches that have access to good amateur musicians who play for free sometimes hire professionals to do a better job and save rehearsal time.

Staff positions are not really in the freelance category except perhaps as part-time work; they do offer employment opportunities for the trained organist, pianist, and choir director.

Dances may be held in church social halls on special occasions, with hired dance bands and combos. Remember, however, that while a Catholic church may hire a big band for its St. Patrick's Day dance, the Baptist church down the street may not believe in dancing. Check around before making sales calls.

Rehearsal pianists, especially in larger churches, are needed for extensive choir programs. The pay may be unexciting, but the work should be pleasant and regular.

GOSPEL AND CONTEMPORARY CHRISTIAN MUSIC

Performing gospel and contemporary Christian music allows musicians to practice their religion through music—and make money as well. In some parts of the country this is a very active and expanding market, and both instrumental and vocal groups can find ample opportunity to perform.

Many contemporary performers have adopted their secular competition's style and show-business glitter but see themselves primarily as religious entertainers. Amy Grant, for example, by mid-1985 had collected one platinum and three gold records, and *Newsweek* called her "the first evangelical superstar."

Special concerts in churches, civic auditoriums, schools and colleges, public parks, and even huge tents feature gospel and other religious musical groups. Often these events will engage six or eight different ensembles. At least two national magazines now serve the "popular" religious music market (see Appendix A), and some large cities have one or more radio stations devoted to gospel or contemporary Christian music.

Even though religion may seem far from the business of entertainment, you'll find that success in performing this kind of music requires the same business and show-business skills as does any other area of entertainment. You'll have to organize, book, and play these engagements with the same attention to business detail that every music job requires.

NOVELTY

Novel uses of music are the products of imagination and are perfect examples of the creative approach. The following ideas are for you to consider for your list of possibilities and for stimulating your own imagination. In one way novel jobs are like all others in the freelance music business: they are where you find them—or make them.

The "singing (or playing) telegram" is one new, and growing, market offered by such companies as Eastern Onion and Balloons and Tunes. If you are outgoing and funny, are blessed with creative flair, and have, perhaps, a touch of the bizarre, you could do well here.

Street musicians working in many large cities make an art of making their own jobs. This kind of music offers direct communication between player and audience. If they like your music, you make money. If they don't, you starve.

A cover story on street musicians in *USA Today* (May 1, 1984) tells of such players making "up to $400 a day" and notes that several former street players have become concert or recording artists. (It has been reported that some San Francisco street musicians make well over $30,000 a year; I pass this along without verification.)

According to *People* magazine (July 22, 1985), many cities are now accepting this form of music. Since 1983, Chicago has issued more than 700 street-performance permits. Though many cities do allow—or regulate—street musicians, some don't. "On the street," one player commented, "the police are the ultimate critics."

One especially creative street musician is Grimes Poznikov, who mans a "human juke box" in a San Francisco park; he plays tunes on his trumpet when a selection is made and a coin inserted in the appropriate slot. He is utterly independent, and people enjoy his show (and music) enough to pay. "Basically," he says, "I'm an anarchist."

If you are adventurous and something of a showperson, you might consider this form of contemporary minstrelsy.

Don't be limited to the same old traditional jobs. With novelties in music, you can be as creative as possible. Think of a job to match your talents, and then sell or try out the idea. A trumpet player I know has played more than one wedding fanfare from a hot air balloon hovering over the site of an outdoor ceremony.

MUSIC-RELATED JOBS

Don't overlook nonperforming, but music-related, jobs: You can often profit from your expertise in nonplaying ways. Some of these could even lead to a career or new professional directions for you. Here are a few suggestions; you'll think of others that may better match your talents and interests.

Radio and TV jobs requiring music knowledge include program planning and on-the-air work. If you're a true jazz buff, for example, you might produce a weekly jazz show for a local FM station—or a bluegrass, folk, or chamber-music hour if that's your specialty. Perhaps you could use your expertise in the programming field or even in selling broadcast advertising time.

Music libraries are specialized centers requiring trained librarians. A degree in library science or media-center administration combined with your musical knowledge could start a new career. Currently, there are about 600 music libraries in this country alone.

Music therapy also requires special schooling and certification, but a college degree combined with your performing background might lead to a satisfying career helping people through music. (See Appendix D for more information.)

Music criticism may be satisfying for musicians who also like to write. Local newspapers, magazines, and broadcasting stations all need music critics. If you understand music, the qualities of a good performance, and the essentials of writing clearly, part-time music criticism may get you free tickets, free records (if you write record reviews), *and* a paycheck.

PRIVATE TEACHING

Once you become proficient with your music, why not share your knowledge and skill with others? Teaching music offers a stable way to augment your income and could become your main occupation. But teaching isn't easy. It requires patience, organization, and the ability to demonstrate and explain difficult concepts.

For some kinds of music teaching, college preparation is required, but for other musical styles, professional experience is more important. If you want to teach advanced classical piano, say, you'll most likely need at least an undergraduate degree. If, however, you want to teach improvisation—a skill not always taught in college—you'll need to be an excellent jazz/pop player yourself.

One prominent Atlanta pianist, for example, is more interested in jazz and his own compositions than in pleasing commercial clients. He finds that teaching jazz and improvisation offers him a sizable income without the pressures of performing music he doesn't enjoy. He has fifty students and gets fifteen dollars per half-hour lesson. Because he enjoys teaching, he doesn't mind working in the same studio all day.

To prepare yourself for teaching, you'll need to organize your approach, determine what you have to offer, and attract students. Often you can work with public-school music teachers and music stores to find pupils. Word-of-mouth advertising is the best kind. One satisfied student will quickly lead to another.

How much can you make? How much should you charge? Teaching fees vary widely—depending on where you are, how much education and experience you have, what you teach, and how much competition you have—but most musicians can add significantly to their income by taking at least a few students. Find out what other teachers offer and charge, and price your services accordingly. Read books and magazine articles on music teaching to get more ideas on this important aspect of professional music. (See Appendices A and B for further reading.)

TECHNICAL ASSISTANCE

Technical assistance is increasingly significant to musicians because electronics, sound reinforcement, and computers are now an important part of the music world.

Only a few years ago, for example, a pianist was just that—a pianist. He or she would simply walk in, sit down at the house piano, and play. Today, even the name has changed. The term is now likely to be "keyboard player" or even "synthesist," and familiarity with electronics, synthesized sound, and computers may be as important to the performance as musical ability.

Musicians who are technically inclined and trained and who understand these newer aspects of the business may find many jobs waiting for them.

Younger or less experienced players might find "roadie" work a good way to gain experience. Carting electric pianos, guitars, and drums or setting up and running sound equipment should not be left to non-musicians.

Sound reinforcement is an increasingly important area of contemporary music. The way a group sounds can depend more on the sound engineer than on the players themselves. This is true for classical ensembles as well as rock performers. Even beginning local bands often depend on a sound specialist to keep the sound "right" out front.

Teaching electronic music techniques is a new opportunity for those who understand changing technologies. Synthesists, for example, may find work teaching other keyboard players how to program their new instruments. Since many pianists are confused and frightened by the new wave of electronics, enterprising synthesists will probably find many students if they can share their knowledge.

Synthesizer programmers can also find work in recording studios or at special promotions in music stores and at trade shows. Some synthesizer masters create and sell programs on cassette tape—ready to be loaded into the memory of popular synthesizers—and they advertise this service in national music magazines. This is a perfect example of enterprising musicians taking advantage of changing technology.

REPAIR SERVICES

Instrument repair is another promising area for technically minded musicians.

The traditional fields of band-instrument repair and piano tuning are excellent sources of steady work for qualified technicians, and the repair field is expanding because of the new, complex electronic equipment now being widely used. The musician who can repair amplifiers, electronic keyboards, and related equipment will be in demand.

Instrument and equipment repair is not, of course, a strictly musical skill, and many repair people are not musicians at all. However, musicians who are competent at repair work will have a distinct advantage, since they will be able to communicate directly with their customers and understand exactly what is needed.

Musicians who are interested in electronics and technology may find that technical schools in their areas offer low-cost or free training in electronics. This schooling and subsequent work won't interfere with night music jobs and can open new career doors for technically adept musicians.

SALES

You know you'll have to sell your own music to make money from it. That's what this book is all about. But selling yourself and your music is not the only profitable way to combine music with selling. Becoming a music salesperson, part time or full, is another.

If you enjoy working with people, you might enjoy sales, as well. So consider:

● Selling in a music store. Many of today's instruments are so complex that knowledgeable salespeople are in demand. If you understand synthesizers, for example, why not get a job demonstrating and selling them? You'll acquire steady daytime income, stay up-to-date on new developments, and get a discount on your own purchases.

● Selling in record stores and sheet-music shops offers the same advantages. Your specialized knowledge of the field will make you especially valuable to the store manager, and you'll get a chance to increase your involvement with music.

An extra benefit is that a music store is often a center for a community's musical activity, so you'll keep up with what's going on with bands, musicians, and jobs in your area.

Most music stores are locally owned, and you can deal directly with the owner or manager. You may also find selling jobs through employment agencies or the want ads. Describe your musical background, but concentrate on your selling abilities—even if they're unproven. Music-store owners, like nightclub managers, are more interested in profits than in musical ability.

Never sold anything? Don't think you could? Don't worry. If you're interested in this field you can develop selling skills. Many excellent and inspirational books teach sales techniques (see Appendix B for suggestions).

WRITING, ARRANGING, AND COPYING

Writing, arranging and copying can be a lucrative sideline for many freelance musicians. Depending on your talent and skill, there are several kinds of writing that you may do:

Writing lead sheets for soloists, vocalists, bands, or shows is a much-needed talent. (Lead sheets are transcriptions of individual songs, with only the melody line and supporting chords indicated—a bare minimum that leaves interpretation up to the performer.) This may involve simply transcribing melodies and chords from records. Or it may require working with composers who don't read music. Singers, particularly, need lead sheets in their keys, and this is an area where a bit of expertise will be lucrative. Since there is a steady supply of new bands and vocalists who need lead sheets of current tunes, this market can provide a dependable part of your income.

Writing full arrangements, scores, and shows is a much more challenging field and usually requires special schooling and study. Good arranging skills are rare, and a freelancer who is a gifted composer/arranger may have as much work as he or she can handle. Typical jobs include writing shows for vocalists and bands, creating special arrangements or scores for audiovisual productions and movies, and compoosing advertising jingles.

It is not uncommon for a player who writes a little to evolve into a writer who plays a little. Good writers and arrangers in such a specialized field as advertising-jingle writing may make much more money than the players who record their music.

Copying the music that others write requires a meticulous mind and close attention to detail. Good copyists, particularly in large cities, can make substantial incomes, though synthesizer-computer-printer technology may eventually have a substantial impact in this field.

If you enjoy calligraphy, are creative with pen and ink, and know music well, you might augment your income through copying. Certainly, every musician who plays a clear, well-written chart will thank you.

Songwriting is not—at least for the beginner—a dependable way to make money. It does offer the chance to write hit songs and collect royalties for a long time. That possibility, however, is fairly remote because of the enormous number of people diligently writing and submitting songs. Don't quit your job to become a songwriter, but if you like to compose music or write lyrics, be persistent. It's hard to get started, but once your name is known, you'll be able to get your work heard.

Some excellent, very helpful books and magazines for songwriters are suggested in Appendices A and B, and many songwriters' clubs offer support, suggestions, and recognition.

RECORDING

To many people, *recording* means record albums, hit songs, the quest for gold or platinum records, and the fast-lane world of the pop celebrity. The record industry is, to be sure, a large and very visible part of the music world, but recording fortunately can mean much more than striving for hit records.

The desire to make a big record is natural, but the chances for success are remote. Sid Bernstein, a widely known New York record producer commented in a 1984 interview that a *fantastic talent* with a *fantastic demo* has about a 6,000 to 1 chance of getting an album deal, which is merely the beginning of the road to recording success. Pursuing this avenue requires a heavy investment; the necessary video may cost $10,000 for a bargain-basement production, and a decent album itself could be another $70,000 to $100,000. Worse yet, these expenses are not paid by the record company.

But as depressing as the odds against recording a hit record may be, there is plenty of other work in the recording industry for all kinds of musicians. Since this market is expanding, all musicians should think of recording as a potential market. Demos, jingles, locally produced records, audiovisual and movie scores, video production, multimedia concert events—all are growing markets for recorded music.

This is an area where changing technology is having a rapid impact. Advanced, compact, and less expensive recording equipment has recently made it possible for smaller cities and towns to have excellent recording facilities. More recording studios mean more work for musicians everywhere. No longer is recording the exclusive domain of New York, Nashville, and the West Coast.

There are several different kinds of recording sessions.

Jingles are musical commercials for businesses, nonprofit organizations, and government agencies. The money, time, and energy spent on a thirty- or sixty-second commercial may be unreal in every sense, but the musician's job is to do just what is asked. Never mind that the extremely difficult part you play may be inaudible in the final mix when the voice-over is complete!

On the other hand, you may help produce an award-winning and popular jingle that becomes part of the consciousness of every American who watches TV or listens to the radio.

Payment for playing in jingle sessions ranges from fairly low for local, limited-use spots to extravagant for union players and singers who receive residuals for long-running national commercials.

You may find that the recording musicians in your area form an informal clique, and it may be difficult to get started in this potentially lucrative area. If you aspire to this kind of work, however, it will be worth your while to keep trying to become a regular player on jingle sessions.

Demo sessions produce demonstration tapes of some sort—perhaps for a songwriter, a singer, or a band. Since these tapes are usually financed by one person (a songwriter, for example) rather than a company, the pay may be quite low. Demo sessions, however, provide a lot of work for studios and musicians and can lead to more important, higher paying studio jobs.

Almost every small town now has at least an eight-track studio and often will support several larger enterprises. The commercial recording market will continue to grow and will rely increasingly on freelance musicians to provide music for a variety of needs.

Record sessions usually take place in established recording centers, and the pay is set by union scale (American Federation of Musicians or American Federation of Television and Radio Artists). Studio players in major cities are among the most competent, accomplished, and best-paid musicians anywhere. Consequently, this area is among the most difficult markets for most players to enter. However, even if you never play a record session in Los Angeles, you may be needed locally by entertainers and groups who are making their own albums or videos.

Miscellaneous recording work includes production of audiovisual and film scores, recordings for sales meetings, and music for television shows. A large company, for example, may want upbeat, exciting music to enliven its awards presentations. Rather than depend on hiring a live band in Hawaii—or Jamaica or wherever its sales meetings are held—the company decides to use recorded music. Or a comedian may want to record backup music because his budget won't always support a live band. Such recording sessions are typical of a local studio's work, and the variety can be as stimulating as if a platinum album were the goal.

All freelance players who are capable musicians and good readers—and who understand different styles—should stay in touch with nearby studios. There may be few calls for a bassoonist, but when a bassoon is needed, nothing else will do.

Recording work is an excellent goal for all musicians, and it can be exciting and well paying. In many cases, however, only the best, most versatile, and most persistent musicians will be able to find work regularly in demanding studio settings. Highly developed playing skills are often required.

You must have so mastered your instrument that you can play whatever is set before you—and play it well. Most recording sessions allow little rehearsal time—maybe once or twice through the part—so excellent sight-reading is essential. Music on tape is unforgiving. Intonation problems, rhythmic inaccuracies, or other lacks of precision will be painfully obvious. Nothing is as embarrassing as making the mistake that requires another "take," causing more work for everyone and costing the client more money in studio time.

In some recording sessions, "head charts" are used. These are very rough sketches instead of completed arrangements. There may be no written music at all. In such sessions, your ability to improvise is critical. You also should be adept in many styles. The producer may ask the pianist, for example, to try a Donald Fagan-style sound—or Billy Preston, or Erroll Garner, or virtually anyone. In these situations, the pianist would be expected to know—and be able to provide—whatever style the producer wants. Sometimes you may even make "record copies" and need to reproduce exactly the tunes that are hot at the moment.

Because studios normally charge by the hour, mistakes caused by becoming rattled under pressure can be expensive and incur the wrath of the producer or the client. Nervousness in the recording studio is taboo. Instead, you need to be relaxed and self-assured.

BOOKING

What if you get several calls for a band on a busy Saturday night? Should you simply tell the callers that you're already working? Why not do a little booking yourself?

If you're well organized, know enough musicians, and attend properly to details, you can add "part-time booking agent" to your list of freelance opportunities. To book a group occasionally, you'll line up the musicians, send the contracts, double-check with the client and the bandleader, and collect a commission. On a smaller scale, you could agree on a finder's fee or referral charge with other musicians, say, twenty-five dollars for each job you refer.

Probably the most useful attribute a booking agent can have is the ability to sell, to talk easily with people, to persuade. In this area of the music business, selling ability is much more important than playing talent. If you are outgoing and like selling, you may do very well as an agent. (See Appendix B for further reading on selling.)

Should you want to start a full-time booking agency, you'll soon realize that it's nearly mandatory to have prior experience in this competitive field. Try, therefore, to work for an established business before striking out on your own. As with any business, you'll have to deal with business licenses, zoning permits, bookkeeping, taxes, and other details. Booking as a full-time job may look easy, but it isn't.

Hard work or not, you can make quite a bit of money in this area of the business. If you book all the entertainment for a convention with a $50,000 entertainment budget, your commission should be several thousand dollars. Furthermore, if you regularly book players for weddings, receptions, or other events, you could easily make an extra one or two hundred dollars weekly.

If you're just starting, try to get a job—clerical, secretarial, or sales—with an established agency to learn how the business operates. For a full-fledged booking business, an extensive network of contact people, both in music and in every part of the business community, is essential to generate a substantial amount of work.

NOW TAKE TIME OUT TO REVIEW YOUR LIST

You should now have many entries on your list of jobs possibilities, and your own compilation is probably quite different from this one. Yours might be longer, or shorter, and it might include jobs that aren't discussed here at all.

Now is not the time to be exactingly critical of your list. It is the time, however, to review your list to see if you have followed the guidelines stated earlier. Here are a few questions to keep in mind as you look back over your ideas for jobs that need your music:

● Have you written down every job idea you yourself might possibly handle—no matter how apparently outlandish or far fetched—or even silly—it seems?

● Have you brainstormed for new uses for your music, or have you restricted yourself to ideas listed in this book?

● Have you practiced your association techniques to expand your list to include similar, but new, uses for your music?

● Are the entries relevant to your own instrument(s), musical tastes, and ability?

● Have you limited your list to the kinds of jobs you have already played, or have you branched out, expanded your horizon?

Opportunities in music go far beyond playing in clubs, in churches, or at concerts. As you work on your Job Possibilities list, add nonplaying, but music-related, items like those mentioned or ones you dream up. The idea, once again, is to create as broad a market list as you possibly can. Maybe your interests will direct you toward music therapy or broadcasting, for example. Perhaps you will have to get a degree to achieve your ultimate ambition. But you'll be working with music and working toward a goal. It's hard to beat that combination.

The Job Possibilities list you have made and are about to review is yours and yours alone. You are going to use it later as a worksheet for planning exactly how to market your musical wares. The list you finally end up with will be the one you use to find work, create jobs, and earn more money for yourself. Better that your list is too long than too short, for the idea you discard today might appeal to you tomorrow.

While you review your list—mostly to see what you've omitted—let your mind roam. See if you can invent a new use for your music—create a need as the advertisers sometimes do—and highlight it on your ever-expanding list of possible jobs.

11

Your Best Possibilities

Now you should have a long list of possible jobs that could use your music. You have really tried to go beyond the same old routine engagements that you've always played, because creativity and flexibility are necessary to keep up with the changes in your community. You also know that the more possibilities you've listed, the more jobs you'll be able to book.

Think for a while about the lists you've been working on. There's no rush, no compulsion to finish today, and you'll probably do a better job if you take it easy. Think about your lists for several days, particularly the Job Possibilities list that requires your creativity. Mull them over. Sleep on your ideas and see if you can expand on what you have.

Remember that the list process used in the creation of your PMMS is not a one-time thing. Your lists should continue to grow with your music and professional life, and you'll be coming up with new uses for your music as long as you play. The PMMS, if used creatively, should be a long-lasting guide for your music-marketing efforts.

WORK SMARTER, NOT HARDER

When you put your Personal Music Marketing System into action by compiling a list of top job prospects, complete with names and addresses, you will probably be surprised at the number of potential clients you develop. For each job category you may have eight or ten—or as many as forty or fifty—names of people who need to know about your musical abilities.

One way to keep your work load manageable, and to use your time most efficiently, is to start with the most likely clients, those whose needs closely match your talents. You may end up calling on every single potential client you can think of in every category you've developed, but you'll work smarter if you start with the best prospects.

You have spent time brainstorming, trying to come up with unusual or outlandish ideas for selling your music. Now is the time to go through your lists to pick out the best prospects. Save all your ideas, of course, even the unlikely or impractical ones, but start your efforts where you have the best chance for success.

MATCH THEM UP

Go through both lists now, and see if you can draw any conclusions about your best job possibilities by comparing your personal music inventory with your job ideas lists. First, read back over your personal inventory and note your strong points and most-developed talents. Then, check your Job Possibilities list and note which ones make best use of such strong points. You might put a star by those listings or underline them in red. When that's done, transfer them to the Best Possibilities Worksheet included in this chapter. You may need to photocopy this page before you start, to be sure of having enough space, or you may want to use a separate notebook. Either way, you're almost ready to start your final list.

For example, if you're a trumpet player, and sight reading is at the top of your list of well-developed skills, your best job possibilities could include playing shows, work at recording studios, freelancing with local symphonies, and church concerts. You'd want to put those job possibilities at the top of your list. Those won't be your only potential jobs, of course, but you'll be most efficient if you start with the jobs you play best.

Don't discard the idea of playing fanfares at outdoor weddings if that's on your list, but don't make it your top priority, either.

Here's another example. If yours is a chamber-music group, your best job prospects might include educational work at schools, concerts in various places, recording, and even society work in homes or at exclusive parties. Thus, you'd rank these as your prime possibilities. Keep all the other ideas for use as you market your music, but plan your efforts to start with the most likely, the best prospects, and work down from there as time permits.

As you rank your Job Possibilities list, looking for the best, most likely prospects, consider several factors. Naturally you'll ask which jobs will pay the best, but you should also think about which will be the least trouble to book and play. Decide which offer year-round opportunity and which are strictly seasonal. Consider which are most common in your area and "feel right" to you.

Follow the brainstorming techniques discussed earlier, and use the categories on the worksheet to stimulate your own ideas.

If your specialty, for example, is playing Polish music but there isn't a Polish community nearby, you'd be foolish to put Polish weddings at the top of your list. If Hawaiian music is your main interest and you live in rural Kansas, you'll have to temper what you like with what your local market needs.

Don't discard the talent-to-job match-ups that aren't at the top of your list. Later, you'll want to expand your job search beyond your top listings, but it's most efficient to start with your strongest possibilities.

BEST POSSIBILITIES WORKSHEET

Well-Paying Jobs _____

Easy-to-Book Jobs _____

Year-Round Jobs _____

Seasonal Jobs _____

Jobs I'm Already Working _____

NOW ADD THE NAMES AND NUMBERS

Your refined Best Possibilities should now be ranked in order on the list shown on page 99, with the best prospects for your kind of music at the top and the rarer, more unusual, or even experimental potential jobs listed lower. The reality is that you won't have the time or the energy to call on everybody, so you must be selective.

The final step in developing your Personal Music Marketing System is adding names to each category—finding the prospects' addresses and telephone numbers—and each of your categories may yield dozens of names. If you start with your best prospects, you won't be overwhelmed with the sheer number of sales calls that should be made, and your success ratio will be higher.

YOUR GOOD PROSPECTS LIST

The next list in your Personal Music Marketing System will be all-important to your plan of action. It will contain specific names, addresses, and phone numbers of many possible buyers of your music.

Making this list requires a good deal of research, and it will take more time and effort to compile than the other lists. The time you spend finding names and numbers will be very worthwhile, however, because this list will be your blueprint to success in the freelance music business.

The Good Prospects list will be especially useful because it is created with your previous lists as guides. Since those compilations focused closely on the kind of music you do best, your marketing effort will be like a rifle aimed at a very precise target, not like a shotgun blast that would waste your energy searching for clients who don't need your kind of music. The basic sources for names on this list will be:

- *Your experience*
- *The Yellow Pages of your phone book*
- *Newspapers*
- *City and regional magazines*
- *Chambers of commerce, convention bureaus*
- *The* Encyclopedia of Associations *in your library*

The names on this final list will be the people you'll call on to sell your music, so the more good prospects you have, the more you'll be able to sell. Your first lists have been general inventories that you compiled by brainstorming and by using ideas from earlier chapters of this book. The Good Prospects list, however, will be specific and will require basic market research to compile.

Categories for All Freelancers

Let's get started on this final list for your PMMS. There are two general categories of prospects that should be on almost all musicians' lists, and we'll start with these. Other, more specialized job prospects will come from your Job Possibilities list. No matter what instrument you play, however, these potential clients should know what you have to offer:

- *Booking agents, producers, and music brokers*
- *Established bandleaders, contractors, and conductors, depending on your instrument*

Both these categories are important to all freelance players. Even if you think booking agents wouldn't be interested in your Renaissance Music Consortium, there may be a time when a client desperately needs a viola de gamba or a recorder player. *If they don't know you, they won't call you.*

Perhaps the most convenient way to make this list is to use separate sheets of notebook paper for each category and skip a few lines between entries. Remember, paper is cheap. Its cost shouldn't stand in the way of making your list organized and neat. Or you may want to use a separate index card for each potential client.

Maybe you have a computer or some other efficient filing system. Whatever method you use, be sure that you are able to keep up with the information you compile so that you can find and use it as needed.

Let Your Fingers Do the Walking

You already own one of the main resources that you'll use: the Yellow Pages. This annual compilation of businesses, listed by category, will be invaluable. You couldn't afford to buy the information available to you free in this useful book.

There is a skill to the most effective use of the Yellow Pages, particularly in large cities with huge books. Companies must pay the phone company to be listed in more than one category, so you may have to check several headings before your list is really complete.

Agents and producers, for example, will probably be listed under "Entertainment Bureaus" but might also be found under "Convention Services," "Musicians," or several other categories. Be sure, then, to look under each applicable category while you're compiling this list. Use your associating and brainstorming skills to find as many useful categories as you can. Remember, the people who compile the Yellow Pages aren't musicians, so you may have to dig to find the listings you need.

Start your market prospects list, then, by going through the Yellow Pages and entering all the booking agents, music producers, and bandleaders you can locate. Add recording studios to your list if your playing has reached that level. Include phone numbers and addresses.

Virtually every musician should be known by these people, and you should certainly view booking agents as possible clients, no matter what your instrument. Someday the producer at a recording studio, or a local contractor, will need you, but, to repeat, potential clients don't call you if they don't know you!

Define Your Markets

If you live in a small town, or within a megapolis, or near a resort area, you'll also want to consult the Yellow Pages for communities near your own. Include all the potential clients within easy driving distance, and remember that it may sometimes be worth your while to drive a few hundred miles for an extra-special job. Your primary market area should include all cities and towns within, say, a hundred miles, and your secondary market area could extend to two or three hundred miles—even further in some cases.

If you play an unusual instrument, or have an uncommon act, you should enlarge your market area so that anyone who needs your rather rare skill will know of your availability. Thus, double-reed players, operatic tenors, and harpsichordists will probably define their primary market area more broadly than, say, guitarists or drummers.

A bassoonist can certainly count on less freelance music work than a sax player, but the bassoonist will also face less competition, perhaps none. When a recording studio, symphony orchestra, church music director, or theater group within a hundred miles needs a bassoon, there may be only one choice.

So depending on your area, find Yellow Pages for all your target markets. You can find phone books for other cities at your phone company or public library, or you can buy Yellow Pages for any city in the country through your local phone company's business office.

Now Expand Your Market List

Once your list contains names of people and groups from the general categories (that is, agents, producers, recording studios, and bandleaders), you are ready to start personalizing your market list. Now you'll refer to your second compilation, the Job Possibilities list, which contains types of jobs relevant to your music. Still using the Yellow Pages as your primary research tool, go through your Job Possibilities list and find applicable names, addresses, and phone numbers for each type of job you are considering.

You may not find many names of individuals, but company names and numbers will do. At first, just locate company names and numbers to match the categories of possible music jobs from your Job Possibilities list. Later we'll discuss how to find the appropriate contact person at a company.

Watch What Happens

For example, let's say that you are a classical guitarist and that one promising job category in your second list is weddings and receptions. You think that your soothing guitar music could be effectively and profitably used in wedding ceremonies and receptions, and you need to match specific names with this idea. You have the Yellow Pages in hand. Where do you look? In this case, you start with the wedding category. You probably will find:

Wedding chapels. Obviously, the owners and operators of these chapels should know what you could do for their clients, so add them to your prospect list.

Wedding consultants. These are wedding planners, and they should be at the top of your list. Many will be women operating from their homes, some will be florists, others may be photographers. You can be sure that they are very much into the wedding business, and they should certainly learn of what you can offer their clients.

Wedding receptions. This listing may refer you to "Caterers" and "Banquet Rooms." Both categories should be added to your list. Anyone connected to the wedding business must be informed of your availability to play classical guitar music at weddings and receptions.

Wedding supplies and services. This category includes rental companies, photographers, card shops, printers, and any other kind of business that could be important to a prospective bride and groom. You'll want many of these people to know of your musical availability. Some of them keep card files or bulletin boards on which you might display your card or promotional literature. In return, offer to recommend *their* services when possible and ask for their cards. You might even want to work out a reciprocal referral or finder's fee arrangement with other business-people in the field. You might send them twenty-five dollars, or even ten percent of every job you book from their referrals.

Now, follow up by looking under the cross-referenced suggestions for "Caterers" and "Banquet Rooms."

Caterers. Here you'll have to filter through all the listings to find those that specialize in weddings and similar functions. Obviously you should not spend time calling on the local barbecue spot or a fast-food restaurant that lists itself as a caterer, but concentrate on those listings that could be good wedding prospects.

Banquet rooms. Large restaurants, hotels, and meeting halls are listed here. Most hotels will insist on providing the food for affairs held in their facilities, so adding them will not duplicate your "Caterers" list. Use your discretion and don't list so many places that you'll be dumb-founded by the number of sales calls to make; list only the most promising prospects.

Florists and photographers. You noticed many listings for these businesses in the "Caterers" category, so check these two categories separately in the Yellow Pages. Besides, you'll find several businesses specializing in weddings that were not included elsewhere. Add them to your list.

You still aren't finished using the Yellow Pages to locate possible clients for your classical guitar playing. Next look at the listings for:

Churches and synagogues. You should contact ministers,

rabbis, organists, directors of music, and social activities directors, especially if you live in a smaller town with fewer caterers and wedding consultants. Since you play classical guitar, you won't be viewed as inappropriate or as competition to the staff organist. You may not get many jobs from these contacts, but you should receive enough referrals to make at least an introductory visit or call worthwhile.

Tents. Many wealthy people rent large, expensive tents for wedding receptions on the lawn. If they can afford to have a party under an expensive tent, they certainly can afford you, so contact the rental companies that provide for these parties. If you are on good terms with them, they'll give you good leads.

Rental services. This category includes companies that rent formal wear, as well as those that provide party supplies. Get to know these businesspeople, and you'll expand your sources of wedding leads and tips. Leave a few of your cards with these companies.

This example should show you how useful the Yellow Pages can be. You'll probably find even more listings for the job categories that interest you, especially if you live in a large city. You are looking for names and numbers to call on, and the Yellow Pages will be a continuing resource. In fact, it might be better to call the Yellow Pages the "Gold Pages" because they offer so much valuable information.

You, the classical guitarist in our example, now have numerous specific names on your list, all from the Yellow Pages. At this point, you have listed names and numbers for these potential clients:

Booking agents	*Caterers*
Musical producers	*Banquet rooms*
Production companies	*Florists*
Recording studios	*Photographers*
Bandleaders	*Churches*
Wedding chapels	*Synagogues*
Wedding consultants	*Tents*
Wedding suppliers	*Rental services*

When you see all these prospects listed, you may feel overwhelmed at the number of potential buyers you've found. But just as valuable as any specific wedding lead is the network of referral sources you've discovered.

You've now researched only one category, weddings and receptions, from your Job Possibilities list, but you've found fifteen different kinds of job contacts within that one category—probably over a hundred names of individual prospects—just from using the Yellow Pages.

This, then, is the way to find jobs. Do your market research, and you will be astounded at the number of prospects for your music. All it takes is a little work—and you know that many of your competitors are still in bed asleep.

Let Your Fingers Do the Walking, Continued

From the example above, you see that the Yellow Pages can really be a gold mine of job prospects for you. Continue working with this list, the Good Prospects compilation, matching the job types on it with all the listings you can find in the Yellow Pages. If you are interested in substitute teaching, look under "Schools and Colleges," "Nursery Schools," "Private Schools," and "Music Stores." If you've listed electronic instrument repair as a strong possibility, check all the listings under "Music Stores," "Music Instrument Repair," "Electronics," and so on. Be sure to use any cross-references that are given and look in all possible categories for company names and numbers.

With more-general categories, such as businesses and public-relations firms, you may have to be more selective in what you put on your Good Prospects list. In major cities with large business communities, you'll want to limit your efforts to excellent prospects—the largest, or the most prosperous, or the best known, or the most specialized companies in any given field. On the other hand, if you live in a small town or rural area, or if your music is unusual or esoteric, you may have to list every single job possibility you can locate.

In any case, the Yellow Pages will be a continuing and valuable source of job prospects, and you should start your market research with this easy-to-use, always available, and up-to-date source. When you have exhausted the information in the Yellow Pages, you'll probably have more names of potential clients than you could possibly use.

But wait! You have only just begun.

GOOD PROSPECTS WORKSHEET

	Company	*Address*	*Telephone*

Booking Agents

Music Producers

Recording Studios

Bandleaders

Convention Services

Add Your Own Headings

12

Contact People

You're making good progress. For your PMMS you've come up with all kinds of interesting ways of playing music for pay. You've perhaps actually invented several jobs and thought up parties that just won't work without your own special music. You have your Good Prospects list well under way; it will never be completed but added to and modified as conditions change in the music world and you gain experience in marketing your music. You're almost ready to activate that Good Prospects list and put it to work for you.

The big question remains. Who will hire you? Who will your clients be? The people you work for will vary, most likely, from a busy mother who's planning a wedding reception to the president of a large corporation. Part of the excitement of the freelance life is that you don't have to do the same thing every day. You welcome the challenge of new jobs, new faces, new clients.

Even so, you'll probably find that much of your work comes through certain well-established channels. It will pay you to get to know these people, understand what they expect, and learn how they operate. You'll be more comfortable, and so will they.

Sometimes it will be appropriate for you to pay a referral or finder's fee to the person who recommends you. Discuss this possibility with those who are in a position to send a lot of business your way. Perhaps you could send a check for twenty-five dollars or even fifty dollars for each job you book through a particular referral source. Remember that when florists or photographers or party planners recommend you, their reputation is on the line almost as much as yours is. The referral fee is a way of thanking them concretely for having confidence in your work.

As long as you do a good job for the client, a referral fee is perfectly acceptable. However, if the quality of your music is poor, then the referral-fee arrangement becomes suspicious, and the referral may have more to do with the fee than with the quality of the musical product. Be sure that you actually do superior work for the client, and everyone will be happy.

There is a lot of overlapping in these categories, just as there probably is in your own marketing lists. Obviously, a hotel's sales staff will be involved in booking weddings, sales meetings, conventions, and many different functions, and meeting planners will work with conventions, trade shows, annual meetings, and other special events.

When you begin to find the same name appearing over and over on your Good Prospects list make sure that you contact that prospect. And when you make those sales calls, be sure to cover *all* of that prospect's interests. Don't just tell a meeting planner about your great convention show; also tell her about your dance band, and your dinner music capabilities. Be specific with prospects—and they'll soon be clients.

PROSPECTIVE CLIENTS

People to contact may fall into many categories. Some are obvious, some less so.

Booking Agents

Booking agents are essentially music salespeople and make their living by matching clients with the kind of music that's requested. Since agents are so important to most musicians, Chapter 14 discusses them more thoroughly.

Agents take a commission from the client's payment, ranging from 10 percent to 30 percent—or more. There are a few national companies with offices in major cities, but most booking agencies are much smaller, with a few salespeople and a limited clerical staff. Often you'll deal with a one-person agency or with an account executive at a mid-size agency.

Some of these businesses specialize in one kind of entertainment. You should learn which agencies are most likely to need your music and strive for a good relationship with them. However, since virtually every type of music job discussed in this book can be booked through an agency, it wouldn't hurt for you to know all the agents in your area.

Many large national agencies are concerned with famous entertainers and very affluent clients. They may occasionally need small local groups, however, so if you live in a resort area or a busy convention city, you should contact out-of-town agencies to let them know what you can provide. A New York agency may book a job in Oklahoma City, and if it has your promo material, it may hire you directly. Or it may work through a local agency.

Remember, booking agents are not interested in art. Booking agents are interested in money, and the client has it. When you talk to agents, emphasize what you can do to make clients happy. Most agents are more interested in your entertainment sense than your perfect pitch.

The Yellow Pages will list agents under "Entertainment Agencies," "Booking Agencies," or "Musicians." A few national agencies are listed in Appendix C.

Convention Planners

Businesses that plan conventions are common in large cities that host many conventions, and they try to provide complete service to their clients. They arrange transportation, food, lodging, tours—and entertainment. If you can meet the regular needs of the convention industry for hospitality, dinner, dance, and show music, you'll find that convention planners will rely on you.

Many such companies are local and small, serving regular clients. They may book music directly or work through an entertainment agency. Sometimes tour companies will expand to provide convention service. These people know far ahead of time who's coming to town, when, and for how long; the type of program being planned; and the possibilities for using music. You'll soon discover that most, but not all, convention work is booked through agents, and you'll learn which agents need your constant attention.

If you can make helpful suggestions during the planning stage (which will be months or years before the meeting), you'll find that your ideas are welcomed. Convention planners and booking agents can get in ruts, too, and your innovative suggestions, especially if they relate to the theme or location of the meeting, can result in more work for you. Note, please, that this applies to practically all convention events needing music. Present your ideas and suggestions early enough to be acted on.

Some planners will add your fees into their overall charge to the client and pay you as a subcontractor. Others will simply refer you to the client and have you make your own contractual arrangements. In this case you may want to pay a "finder's fee" to the person who refers the job to you.

The Yellow Pages list convention planners under "Convention Services," "Meetings," or "Tour Directors." Of the few large national companies, most prefer to work through local booking agencies rather than contacting and hiring musicians directly.

Caterers

Busy caterers know more about the social scene in a community than almost anyone else, so stay in touch with them. Often a caterer will have a years-long association with a wealthy family, or a company, and plan all its party needs, from flowers to entertainment.

If you can become well known to the established caterers in your area, you're apt to get many job leads. Even if your music is out of the ordinary, a creative catering company might very well need it for an unusual kind of party.

Catering companies can be large and well established, with permanent facilities and large staffs, or they can be mom-and-pop operations with little capital. Many caterers operate out of their homes and rent all the necessary equipment for each job. Some specialize in one kind of event—wedding receptions, for example. Get to know them all and offer to pay a referral fee for leads that result in jobs.

Wedding Consultants

If your kind of music lends itself to weddings, you'll need to know the people in your community who are in the wedding business.

Many photographers, florists, formalwear shops, and consultants make most of their income from weddings.

Wedding consultants, who are at the center of all this activity, often recommend musicians to prospective brides and grooms. If they can recommend you with confidence, you'll have a valuable resource for finding work.

These consultants are often one-person companies, frequently working from home. You'll find them under "Weddings" in the Yellow Pages. Many large department stores, formalwear shops, florists, and photographers also offer wedding-planning services, so include them in your list.

Remember that the wedding consultant business is built, like your own, on referrals and on reputation. If you do a good job, you'll find lots of work from this source. If you aren't dependable, though, or don't play appropriate music, wedding consultants will delete you from their referral lists. When you take a job through a referral, remember that not only is *your* reputation on the line, but also that of the person who recommended you. Do your best to uphold his or her faith in you.

Businesses

This is a large category that includes both small, owner-operated companies and the largest corporations in the country. What they have in common is that they use music for certain specific purposes and that they are interested mostly in the "bottom line."

When you deal with small businesses, you'll talk directly with the owner or the manager, and it's usually pretty clear what kind of music is needed and whom you have to please. If the person who hires you is also the person who writes the check, you know who the boss is.

Many large companies have their own staff of meeting planners, sometimes called the protocol department. These people may be in charge of all the company's functions, from elegant receptions to huge stockholders' meetings.

Establishing contacts within some large companies is difficult, even challenging. The person who hires you is often a junior officer or a lower-level manager; as a result, you have the problem of figuring out not only what your immediate contact wants, but what his or her boss wants as well. In many corporate settings, office politics are overwhelmingly important, and you usually don't know who the players are. Furthermore, many people with different musical tastes and entertainment preferences may have to be pleased: the person who hired you, his or her superior, and, not infrequently, several more levels of bosses.

So, when the twenty-seven-year-old junior executive who hired you to play top-forty music tells you not to play any more current tunes at a company dance, it may really be the seventy-eight-year-old president of the company who issued the order. The junior executive's ultimate interest is in making his top boss happy.

Sales meetings may be planned by a vice president or director in charge of sales. When large companies are trying to motivate their sales forces, it sometimes seems that money is no object. One well-known computer company refers, for instance, to its sales meeting expenditures as "dumping money." Take care, then, that you don't *underprice* your music. You can always bargain downward. Some corporations don't feel that they are getting their money's worth unless the bill is high!

Another financial point you should understand when pricing your music for large businesses is that many companies prefer to spend lavishly on business meetings and company events rather than pay the money in taxes. Do your best to help.

Get to know the meeting-planning staffs of all the large companies headquartered in your area. You may be surprised at the range of occasions for which they need music. Businesses entertain in much the same way as individuals do, just on a larger scale, and their meeting planning, or protocol, staff can be a valuable contact for you.

Associations

Many associations have a professional staff of meeting planners, and you should call on them if they're in your community. Some groups will rely on volunteers from the membership, and you'll need to locate the entertainment or program chairperson to offer your services. Other contacts will be the same as those discussed under "conventions."

Civic, Social, and Nonprofit Organizations

A few civic groups, such as the Elks and Moose clubs, have full-time managers for their meeting places, and you should call on them. Other organizations are run by committees of members; let them know what you can offer. Watch the newspaper for information about these events. File names and dates for next year's sales calls if you're too late this year. Many nonprofit organizations have permanent fund-raising staffs; contact the director in your area.

Government Jobs

Find out if your city, county, or state has a cultural-affairs office. If so, get in touch, and find out what they do. Also, if your state has a statewide arts council which may include both government and private members, determine its involvement in producing special festivals and fairs. Your state's tourism board probably publishes a detailed calendar of special events, including sponsors' names and addresses. Your congressional representative can put you in touch with people familiar with National Park Service programs and the music needs of the armed forces. Club managers or entertainment directors at officers' clubs will know their own specific needs. Your reference librarian can help you locate sources of grant, loan, or scholarship money.

Nightclub Jobs

Usually the club owner or manager hires musicians, though some clubs have a music director. Larger clubs and hotels often hire exclusively through an agency, and bands may rotate on a company circuit. Some agencies work exclusively with nightclubs and book only certain kinds of bands, so try to find agencies whose specialties match yours. Current demo tapes will be helpful, and you'll have to audition to book many club jobs. Up-to-date promo material, including recent photos and reviews of your group, will also impress club owners and managers.

Restaurant Jobs

Usually you'll deal with the owner or manager to book jobs in restaurants. Some chains or larger establishments have entertainment directors, often musicians themselves. Of course, booking agents frequently handle placement of musicians in these positions, and private parties will often hire their own entertainment or rely on the restaurateur's suggestions.

Hotel Music

Staff turnover in many hotels is high, so your carefully cultivated contact person may suddenly disappear—or turn up at another hotel. You'll need to stay in touch with entertainment directors, catering and sales staffs, and, in smaller properties, the general manager. Occasionally there will be an entertainment director, usually a bandleader, who books all the hotel's music needs. Often, of course, hotels deal exclusively with entertainment agencies. Private parties and conventions frequently book their own music independently of the hotel.

Substituting

Normally, the musician for whom you are subbing will hire you directly; occasionally, however, the bandleader, or even the booking agency will call you for work as a replacement. Stay in touch with musicians and be sure you are listed with your local union as being available.

Public Relations and Advertising

Contact specific account executives at advertising and PR firms to suggest music for particular events. Each executive is usually in charge of several projects and will welcome your input. If you are making a "get acquainted" call without specific suggestions in mind, try to see as many creative directors and account executives as possible so they'll know what you have to offer for their future projects.

Remember that most jingles and recorded commercials are developed by advertising agency people, so if you are a writer or arranger, you'll want to make this a prime market.

Shopping Malls

Every large mall will have its own activities or special promotions director in the management office. Often, however, special events are planned by outside public-relations or advertising firms. When making suggestions to individual shops, talk to the owner or manager of smaller shops and with the publicity director of larger stores. Booking agents, of course, may be involved in providing entertainment for malls.

Fashion Shows

To book fashion-show engagements, talk with modeling and entertainment agencies, and publicity departments or the buyers at department stores, boutiques, and merchandise marts. Often shopping malls, country clubs, and large restaurants will sponsor their own fashion shows, so stay in touch with their entertainment directors and publicity people. Occasionally, schools and other nonprofit organizations will sponsor annual fund-raising shows.

Clubs

To book club engagements, see the club manager or social-activities director. Some clubs are run by committees, so you'll call on them. Special events are often planned by temporary committees or appointed directors. Many organizations have a social committee, and you should contact its chairman or chairwoman to offer your services. Since the people handling organizational activities often change each year, you'll have to update your list of contact names frequently.

Private Parties

To locate and book parties in homes, you'll need to become well known to the influential party givers in your area. You can contact them directly from notices in the society pages of your local paper or indirectly through booking agencies, caterers, party-supply rental companies, or florists. This is an area where word-of-mouth advertising works best, so build your reputation and freely hand out your cards to likely prospects.

Shows

Large road shows usually book local players through a contractor, leader, or agency. Theaters have music directors or committees. To find work at theaters, talk to the director, producer, or musical director. To book your own show, contact agents and meeting planners, convention consultants, and other musicians.

Circuses, Traveling Shows, and Sports Events

Road shows like the circus will usually carry a few key players and a conductor and pick up other musicians locally. Stay in contact with leaders and contractors for this work. Sports contacts include team publicity people, stadium management, college athletic departments, and public-relations companies. You may be able to book yourself directly, particularly if you have a strong, entertaining act.

Tourist-Related Jobs

To suggest and book tourist-related jobs, see the entertainment directors of tour-promotion outfits, tourist attractions, theme parks, botanical gardens, and other local attractions. Also call on convention planners and the entertainment committees of local civic clubs and associations. Booking agents, of course, need to know of your abilities and ideas, as do cruise lines.

Orchestral Jobs

Orchestral jobs usually demand auditions or tryouts, notices of which are published in national magazines and posted on music-department bulletin boards. The conductor of community orchestras may hire extra personnel, and knowing the teachers and classical players in your community can lead to jobs. Sometimes the arts section of your newspaper will list upcoming auditions.

Church and Synagogue Work

For substitute church/synagogue work, stay in touch with the permanent staff. Special events may be planned by the youth activities or social director. Full-time positions may be filled by church committees or denominational boards, and ads for vacant positions will be found in such professional magazines as *The American Organist.*

Gospel and Contemporary Christian Music

An informal network of churches, colleges, agents, promoters, radio stations, and recording companies deals with gospel and contemporary Christian music. The average booking agent may rarely need to book such a group and may not even be aware of the size of the religious-music movement. Most work in this area will come through people in churches and related organizations: ministers of music, pastors, concert organizers. It is crucial that musicians interested in this specialized music read the publications in that field. (See Appendix A for suggestions.)

Schools

School-system personnel officers hire full-time staff members, but usually department chairpersons or assistant principals hire substitutes. Teachers in music and drama departments need to know what professional talent is available in the community, and alumni or development offices, which often sponsor fund-raising projects, also need to be kept informed. Student center activity directors can give you information about dances and social events. A reference librarian can help you locate information about grants for the arts.

Fraternal Organizations

Many of these organizations—the ones with houses or offices—will be listed in the Yellow Pages. For the names of other fraternities or sororities in your area, watch the newspaper's social pages and current-events calendars, and contact the club officer quoted in the paper.

Of course, most parties and dances will be planned and handled through the entertainment committee, which changes annually if not each semester. You can get a list of Greek organizations from the dean's office or the division of student affairs at local colleges and schools.

Class Reunions

The school office or college alumni office can direct you to the planning committee for each year's reunion. Once again, you'll be dealing with a committee that may know nothing about booking bands, so part of your job will be educational. Newspaper notices will publicize these reunions, but you must act quickly or the entertainment will already be booked. Since committees change for each reunion year, stay in touch with the school's alumni office to locate specific contacts for each group.

Teaching

To find students for private music teaching, contact other teachers for referrals (particularly if your specialty is different from theirs). Also, let local band and choral directors and school music teachers know what you have to offer. Church music directors may be able to send you students, and so can music stores. Some large music stores offer instruction on their premises, and some cities have privately run schools of music or conservatories that use part-time instructors. Many music stores will let you display promotional material on their bulletin boards, and small ads in the Yellow Pages or leisure-time newspapers will be effective.

Technical Assistance

Roadies, soundpeople, and technical assistants are usually hired by the bands they serve. If the band has a manager, he or she will be the one to see. Be sure that you are known as a technically proficient musician at local studios, music stores, rehearsal halls, and equipment-leasing centers. Concert halls and nightclubs also use sound specialists, so you should stay in touch with them as well as with sound-reinforcement companies.

Repair Work

Technical jobs are found in music stores, electronic repair shops, and factory service centers. Many department stores or music shops offer employment to piano tuners and repair technicians. Frequently this work is done by independent craftsmen who own their own businesses, so contact both large and small repair services.

Writing, Arranging, and Copying

To sell your writing and copying talents, become known at recording studios, ad agencies, music schools and conservatories, and even music stores in your area. Be sure that the musicians union has your name on file and that similar organizations—AFTRA (American Federation of Television and Radio Artists) and the local NARAS chapter (National Academy of Recording Arts and Sciences), for example—know your work.

Songwriting clubs usually need professional arranging help, as do singers and entertainers. Finding this kind of work will depend on knowing the client and getting your talents acknowledged.

Recording Work

To become a frequent player on recording sessions, you'll need to be known by producers and engineers at all the studios in your area—and by writers and arrangers. Other players may recommend you, or advertising agencies that know your talents may request that you be hired to play a session.

Your range of clients is likely to be very broad. You'll probably deal with a wide variety of businesspeople, educators, brides, concert promoters, park managers, public-relations professionals, advertising agencies, and many others as your career grows.

As discussed at the beginning of this book, the key to success in dealing with a large variety of contacts is to remember that for each different client you must faithfully provide the kind of music that he or she explicitly hires you to produce. Figure out exactly what the client wants, and do your best to provide it.

Many times you'll have the difficult task of dealing with entertainment committees. A company Christmas party, for example, may be planned by a group made up of people ranging from the parking lot attendant to the chief executive officer. Your job is to try to please them all. In making presentations to such a diverse group, emphasize your versatility and explain that you are accustomed to dealing with mixed ages, backgrounds, and musical tastes.

In every case, with every client, your ultimate task as a freelance musician is to do what the job requires. That may not be easy, but it will ensure a happy client—and a growing career.

MAKING CONTACT

Use your sales skills and ingenuity to reach the right person, the one who buys music. Sometimes your contact will be obvious, sometimes not. Perhaps you'd like to book your dixieland band at a car dealership for the fall sellathon promotion. Whom do you call?

Simply call the receptionist and ask for the person who's in charge of planning that event. Often that's all it takes, because that person is looking for you, too, even though he or she may not know it yet. If the receptionist connects you with the wrong person, explain what you are doing and ask to be referred to the right extension.

Telephone manners are very important in making contact with potential clients. Identify yourself clearly, and once you've established that you're talking to the person who will be planning the event, say, "I'd like to talk to you about music for your fall sellathon. Is this a good time, or should I call back later?" Never jump right into your sales pitch without this basic courtesy.

You may experience some difficulty in reaching the person you need to talk with in a large corporation, for many secretaries and receptionists are trained to protect their bosses from interruptions and unknown callers. Be prepared to answer "What company are you with?" If your freelance business has a name, state it confidently. Since a corporate name can be more impressive in the business world than your own, you might wish to consider calling your enterprise something like Miami Musical Services, Mary Willis Studio, Melodies Unlimited, or High-Tech Productions.

If you haven't chosen a name for your freelance enterprise, don't fake it. That is, don't make up a name for one-time use. Just tell the receptionist that you're a professional musician calling Mr. Jones to offer your services for the convention XYZ Company is planning. The secretary probably knows about the convention, and she'll know that Mr. Jones needs to hire musicians. By being forthright, you'll often be able to get right through to the person you need to talk to.

You may, on the other hand, experience "the runaround," whereby the first secretary says, "Oh, I think Mrs. Brown's office handles that sort of thing." Then Mrs. Brown's receptionist says, "Perhaps you need to talk with our recreational director," who, it turns out, arranges interdepartmental volleyball games, but hasn't the slightest idea about hiring musicians. Keep cool, remain courteous. Somewhere in the business bureaucracy you'll hit paydirt if you politely ask for help from someone with a particularly friendly voice.

At times, you'll be amazed at widespread incompetence. Occasionally you'll even run across arrogance and rudeness. The key is to keep trying, and remember that you are offering something that potential clients *need*. You're not just wasting their time.

When you have reached the person who actually is in charge of planning the event in question, or hiring the band, it's usually a good idea to try to set up a meeting. Businesspeople are used to meeting clients and will want to size you up. Use the ideas in Chapter 15, "Selling," to make them want to hire you.

Before the meeting, you'll find it useful to send your publicity material to the prospect, along with a short note thanking him or her for talking with you and confirming the time of your sales call. Unfortunately, many businesspeople are basically suspicious of musicians—and vice versa—so a preliminary meeting can be very useful in getting to know each other.

Maintain your Who's Important file as discussed in Chapter 4 so that all the information you've worked hard to gather is available when you need it. You'll never be able to recall all the essential personal and business details if you don't write them down for quick retrieval. Think of your memory as an untrustworthy, temporary file. Use your Who's Important file as a reliable, permanent means for helping maintain viable relationships with contacts and clients.

Your network of contacts and clients should grow with your career—but it won't if you fail to nurture it. Prospects will forget you if you don't keep in touch through gentle reminders of your availability. Former clients may not think of you unless you keep your name in circulation.

There is nothing wrong with asking clients to help further your career and broaden your network of contacts by writing letters of commendation for jobs particularly well done. There is nothing wrong, either, with asking your best clients to recommend you to others. Personal recommendations, written or by word of mouth, are probably the best kind of advertising. Most people familiar with your work will be happy to suggest you to their friends and colleagues who need music. Try to make them feel that by passing your name along they'll be doing their friends—as well as you—a favor. Be sure, of course, that you express your appreciation to everyone who helps your career in this way.

Cultivate your clients. Tap into professional and social networks to expand your base of operation. Above all, keep the lines of communication to all contacts busy, but don't overload them. Unobtrusive persistence is the name of this game.

13

More Market Research

Now your Good Prospects list is well under way from your research in the Yellow Pages. That will be one of your main resources for ideas, names, and addresses, but there are other market-research tools that will help your prospects list grow and stay current.

Keeping your market research active is a career-long goal. Just because you have a couple of hundred names as excellent prospects doesn't mean you can stop working and relax. You must keep up with changes in your community and in the music business.

ARE YOU EXPERIENCED?

Your list should certainly include all the clients for whom you have worked in the past. This means other musicians, agents, and clients

125

themselves. Every businessperson knows that past clients are also the best prospects. *But don't let this mislead you into thinking only of the same old jobs.* Your entire marketing effort is to discover *new clients* and develop *new needs* for your music. So use your past music work as a base, a starting point for expansion.

As you add past clients' names to your Good Prospects list, use the brainstorming and association techniques described earlier to develop new names. Look for similar people who might need your music. Thus, if you have played for the opening of a new bank building for the First United Bank, add other growing banks to your list. If First United needed your music, why can't Second People's Bank & Trust, and Third National use you too? If your barbershop quartet has entertained the local bar association at its annual dinner/dance, add other professional groups to your list—associations of doctors, dentists, psychologists, psychiatrists, accountants, engineers. Similar groups have similar needs and will respect your credentials.

Use your past clients list in three ways:

- *As a core listing of people who have used your music in the past and are likely to need it again. Be sure to keep them up on what you have to offer.*

- *As a mental springboard for coming up with other, similar prospects.*

- *As a source of recommendations. When you have played an exceptionally good engagement, it may be appropriate for you to solicit a letter of recommendation from the client for your files. Later, as you prepare publicity material, a few quotes (or even entire letters) will be very effective.*

NEWSPAPERS

To keep abreast of current activities in your community, read the local papers and city or regional magazines. These provide valuable, up-to-date information.

A newspaper will keep you informed about events that use music, and you should read it every day. The only disadvantage is that the lead time may be too short; the music may have already been arranged by the time the newspaper publishes its story. If this happens with a recurring event such as an annual dance, clip the article and put it in your tickler file for the following year. Then make your first contact eight or nine months before the job. It's better to act too soon than too late.

You will find that the most useful newspapers are the local ones. If your area is served by both a large metropolitan daily and a community weekly, read both to get the full picture of what's going on in your area. Some newspapers aren't local enough for your purposes, and you'll find more usable leads in the *Jackson Argus* than in *USA Today.*

Here are some ways to use your local paper to find situations that could use your music. Again, you'll want to use your Job Possibilities list as a guide.

Weddings, parties, and social events will be covered in the "Society," "Women," or "Lifestyle" sections. If you are trying to book weddings and receptions, you'll find leads from the engagement announcements, though you'll need to act quickly. Also, people who are frequently mentioned in the society "Who's News" columns as party givers certainly need to know who you are.

Notice which country clubs are planning special events and which clubs are most active or about to expand. You might learn of the existence of a new social club through newspaper reading.

Watch the "Social Events" calendar for dances and parties to be given by community, social, and church organizations. Again, while the music may already be booked when the newspaper story appears, you should clip the article, put it in your next year's file, and contact the client six to eight months in advance.

The "Business" section will alert you to all kinds of activities that might benefit from your music. You'll find coverage of upcoming grand openings, ground-breaking ceremonies, new-product introductions, and special promotions. You'll need to move fast in order to book music for these events.

Watch for stories about coming conventions, trade shows, sales meetings, and product promotions. You may find hints about special sales that have specific music tie-ins, or seasonal business activities such as fall new-car introductions that need your music. You'll also find leads concerning executive promotions and retirements, both of which can result in parties that need music.

Pay special attention to the "Who's News" columns that cover business personalities in your area. You'll find important contact names, such as the public-relations firm handling a political campaign, or a newly hired catering director at a major hotel, or a developer planning a new resort for the nearby seashore or mountains. Your alertness should provide extra leads.

By reading the business section, you may even find news that you would expect to hear through the music grapevine but may not. You could learn of a new recording studio in town, of a new restaurant/cabaret, or plans for a street festival to revive part of the inner city.

The Arts and Leisure section will yield news of upcoming concerts, newly formed chamber music groups, auditions and tryouts for community orchestras and theatrical productions, recitals, and nightclub appearances. Your music could be needed in many of these situations. You should keep up with who's doing what and what's going on in the local music community.

You may learn, for instance, that the city's symphony is putting on a series of elementary-school concerts to demonstrate the instruments of the orchestra and introduce the students to classical music.

You could apply this idea to your own kind of music, be it bluegrass, jazz, or medieval church music, and explore the possibility of obtaining a grant or other support for a similar kind of school concert program. The possibilities are almost limitless if you keep your imagination active and keep up with what others are doing. Often, by making a slight change, you can apply an idea to your own situation. When you get a good idea, it doesn't matter if it's original—as long as you act on it.

The "Religion" or "Church" section will alert you to special music events and programs, many of which need professional musical help. If you are too late for this year's performance, make a note to contact the music or choral director for next year's events. Holiday seasons will be particularly active. Also note which churches have the most dynamic music programs, and be aware of how your music might fit in.

The "Sports" pages will keep you up-to-date on athletic events and tournaments that may employ music for awards banquets and dances or preliminary kickoff ceremonies—even pep bands.

The papers you read may or may not have a separate "Education" section, but every newspaper carries stories about education—which school district has just passed a bond issue to expand its band program, which schools are particularly active in promoting ethnic and folk music, which college is planning a homecoming festival.

You might get an idea from using your music in a hospital therapy situation from a feature about that subject. A wire-service story about street musicians or a singing telegram service in another city could inspire you to apply that notion to your own area.

The paper will also help you stay abreast of cultural trends, fads, and changes, and you can direct your career more accurately if you know what is going on. America is an evolving, dynamic society, and the music business changes every day. The static person will soon be left behind.

By keeping up with society's trends, you may be among the first to know that disco is coming in—or going out. You may be able to profit from a new interest in jazz, or folk, or ethnic music. You may need to know about new ways to apply computers to the teaching of improvisation. You could benefit from reading about noontime concerts in downtown parks if you apply that idea to your own situation.

And don't forget that the "Classified" section is a great source for buying and selling instruments and other musical equipment.

In short, a close reading of the local newspaper will prove directly beneficial to most musicians. Read it with a pair of scissors handy, maintain a tickler file of clippings, and add important names to your Good Prospects list. A thorough and imaginative daily reading of the newspaper can make the subscription pay for itself many times over.

Again, it's better to act too early than too late, so make notes in your tickler file six, eight, even ten months in advance for annual events. If there is lots of competition for a particular job, you might even contact the prospect a full year ahead with your get acquainted visit.

MAGAZINES

One of the most interesting recent developments in American publishing is the appearance of many city and regional magazines. Some are published by chambers of commerce; others are strictly independent. Some concentrate on business; others are interested in a region's special style of living. You'll find that both types are interesting and helpful.

Use these magazines much as you would a local newspaper, but remember that magazines have a much longer lead time and rarely have any really fresh news. Most of these magazines are filled with feature stories and personality profiles. You can use both kinds of articles to generate job ideas.

For example, let's say you are reading an article in the winter issue of *Santa Barbara* magazine. You notice an article titled "Casa Palmilla, a Hacienda by the Sea," describing an elegant oceanfront home. The style is Spanish, and your specialty, let's suppose, is classic Spanish guitar music. Obviously you'll need to let the homeowners know that their next party would not be complete without your appropriate music.

Or, for another example, you are reading *Business Atlanta,* and you notice a column called "Meeting Facility Review," which discusses a different hotel or resort each month. The information and names given in this article go straight to your Good Prospects list, and since the hotel reviewed is a new one, you should be able to make a good contact for booking convention work.

DON'T FORGET THE ADS!

Don't overlook the ads. Much time, thought, and money are spent producing them, and you can find out a lot about your area by paying attention to what is being advertised. Perhaps a new hotel is touting its Sunday morning brunch. If the atmosphere is formal, couldn't it use a string quartet? Or if it's a blue jean brunch, wouldn't a jazz trio or folksinger be appropriate?

Maybe a local manufacturer is promoting a new line of patio furniture. You might call on the public relations or advertising department to suggest an early spring display featuring your dixieland band at a local shopping center to introduce the new products.

Use magazine and newspaper ads as *idea producers.* You probably don't need a lift truck or a multiterminal computer system, but if those items are prominently advertised in your city magazine, you could probably find a tie-in for your music. When businesses are spending big bucks promoting products, let them know how you can help.

When you think like a businessperson, you'll realize that music can be very useful in creating a mood or generating excitement, and you'll begin to notice all the kinds of events that your music could help. Newspapers and magazines will provide a continuing source of these ideas for your Good Prospects list. You'll find that reading current periodicals can be just as important to your career as reading music.

CHAMBERS OF COMMERCE AND CONVENTION BUREAUS

Chambers of commerce and convention bureaus can be very useful sources of information to freelance musicians. These organizations promote business activity in your area, and you can learn a lot by using their services.

The most valuable help you'll get from the convention bureau will be a complete listing of all the meetings and conventions that are coming to your area. Understandably, these listings are worth money, and policies vary concerning who can use them. Many convention bureaus won't give nonmembers access to this information, and membership may cost more than you can afford—but it's worth a try.

If you live in a major city with hundreds of annual conventions, you obviously won't have the time or resources to contact all the planners and directors. In this case, work with booking agencies that specialize in convention music. If you live in a small town that hosts only a few conventions and meetings, you should probably contact the meeting planners directly. (They'll most likely welcome your creative suggestions.)

Chambers of commerce try to promote all kinds of business activity, not only conventions. They can provide helpful information about economic activity in your area and can alert you to new industry, community celebrations and events, company expansions, and other occurences that might need your music. Often local chambers publish newsletters or calendars of events that you'll find useful.

If your music is a community resource—say a show featuring the life and works of a local composer—you may find that the chamber of commerce will even be interested in promoting *you*.

LIBRARY RESOURCES

As you continue to find good prospects to match the entries on your Job Possibilities list, be aware of the aid that your local library can give. Librarians, especially those who work in reference departments, have access to unbelievable amounts of information, and you'll find them to be very helpful as you do your market research.

Here are a few ways you can use the library:

● Get to know *The Encyclopedia of Associations,* which will be in the reference department. This is a valuable and up-to-date set of books. It lists all the associations and organizations in the United States (currently almost 20,000), gives their addresses and short descriptions, and often tells where the next annual meetings will be held.

You'll find the geographic volume especially helpful. It lists all the associations in each state, by city, so you can find the names of those in your area. Remember that associations have frequent meetings and social events, and many of them use music.

Another interesting feature is the astounding number of music associations. Currently, more than 150 music-related organizations are listed, from the "Country Music Association" to the "Lute Society of America." All musicians will find this a way of keeping up with activity in their areas of musical interest.

● Your library may subscribe to magazines, such as *World Convention Dates* or *Meetings and Conventions,* that list upcoming conventions around the country. Ask the librarian. If your local convention bureau is too expensive for you to join, look through these magazines for some of the same information. Regional magazines from nearby cities can also help you locate potential clients.

● The library probably has out-of-town telephone books from nearby cities. You will find these useful—particularly the Yellow Pages.

● Clip files are maintained by most libraries. They contain news stories, press releases, annual reports, and assorted brochures pertaining to leading companies and citizens. If you are producing a show with local or historical interest, or if you are looking for information to use in preparing a sales call, these files could be a gold mine. Always ask the librarians for help; you'll save time because they know exactly where to look for all kinds of information.

● Don't forget that books can be very helpful in many ways. For example, before you start making sales calls, you will probably want to read one of the excellent books on sales techniques. Also, to keep up with changes in the tax laws, you can find a current handbook on tax preparation for the self-employed. (Several helpful books in these fields are listed in Appendix B.)

YOUR PERSONAL MUSIC MARKETING SYSTEM IS SHAPING UP

Your Good Prospects list should be quite substantial now that you've researched the information sources discussed in this chapter. Devise reminders to consult these sources routinely: newspapers every day, magazines each issue, the Yellow Pages at least every new edition, convention bureaus and chambers of commerce every three months or so, and the local library depending on how fast it acquires new publications.

You may already have so many names on your Good Prospects list that you can't call on all the people included, but what a problem to have! At least you've proved that you don't have to limit yourself to the same old jobs for the same old clients.

In every community there are many job opportunities for freelance musicians, and the simple market research sources discussed in this chapter will help you find them. If you use these sources to keep up with developments in your community, you'll probably be playing a stimulating variety of jobs as often as you'd like.

Finding jobs is probably your most important task as a freelance musician. You can proceed in a hit-or-miss fashion, as most of your competitors will, and be satisfied with more of the same old thing. Or you can use your Personal Music Marketing System to locate jobs that are matched to your talents, *jobs that need your music.*

It takes a little work, but it's worth it.

14

Working with Agents

Many musicians just want to play music. They know little or nothing about the business side of music or about booking jobs. For such musicians, agents can be very important. In fact, many players book most or all of their work through agencies and never worry about dealing directly with clients.

As this book has shown, however, finding jobs that can use your kind of music is not too difficult, and most musicians can profitably locate work on their own.

Perhaps there aren't any booking agents in your community, or your kind of music is so noncommercial that agents aren't interested. Or perhaps you just like the business aspects of the profession. In these cases, you'll certainly be your own agent, use your PMMS, and pay yourself the commission.

Actually, of course, it's not an either/or situation. Most freelance players work with agents sometimes and book jobs directly on other occasions.

One of the "universal markets" that should be at the top of your Good Prospects list is a listing of all the agents in your community. Even if you do most of your work through your own direct dealings with clients, you need to know, and be known by, booking agents.

Many musicians, particularly those with a little business acumen, resent the agent's role. They ask "Why should that nonmusician get a cut of the money I earn?" Nevertheless, you need agents for two basic reasons. One is that in many areas, particularly large cities, agents control much of the work. Major hotels, for instance, will sign exclusive agreements with booking agents, and all the work for that hotel goes through the agent. If you don't know the agent, you don't get the work.

The second reason that you should work with agents is that they're specialists. Their business is selling music and entertainment, and they should be expert salespeople with highly developed skills. Matching your musical talent with a good agent's sales abilities can result in a potent combination that will be profitable to both of you.

ESTABLISHING A GOOD RELATIONSHIP

Musicians play for many reasons—including fun, artistic expression, and personal satisfaction—but agents are in it for the money. Most agents are 99.9 percent businesspeople, interested in the bottom line. Like other clients, they don't care about your musical soul; they only want to know if they can make money with your music. So you should think of them as you think of other clients and find ways to demonstrate that your music will fill their needs. They must believe that your talent will make money for them when they use their sales skills to find jobs for you.

You'll get best results by finding booking agencies that handle your kind of music and match your temperament and your way of doing business. Some agencies are completely rock/pop oriented, some book only college concerts, some specialize in Jewish weddings and other ethnic functions, and others book primarily large shows for major conventions. Some specialize in the six-night nightclub circuit, while others mainly book traveling shows for armed-forces installations around the world. Other agencies promote superstar-level classical soloists and chamber groups. The variety is as wide as the spectrum of music, and you will have to shop around to find a agent who books the kind of freelance jobs you're looking for.

You should also spend a little time becoming known at agencies whose focus is not on your specialty, because occasionally they may need you. For example, an agency that books primarily rock bands for college dances and parties may sometimes get a call for a harpist to play a wedding ceremony. The agency won't turn down the business just because harp music isn't its specialty, so if that's your instrument, and you have let this agency know of your existence, you'll probably get the job.

The task of finding an agent or agents who will serve you well is already under way. You're well into the search, that is, if you've already compiled your Good Prospects list instead of waiting to do it after reading this book straight through. You still have to determine, of course, which agents would be interested in selling your music—and which ones you'd like to work with.

Once you have found an agency, or several, that will work with you, the following guidelines will help you create and maintain a good relationship:

• Communicate honestly and clearly with any booking agencies you plan to work with. Let them know *exactly* what you can and cannot do. Don't take a job if it is beyond your capabilities or outside your area of competence. You'll only hurt yourself, and the agency won't hire you again.

• Discuss details with any agency you work for. Be sure that you understand where the job is, what time it begins and ends, what dress is appropriate, whether you must take your own piano and sound equipment, how much the job pays, whom to report to, whether you must use the loading dock at the back of the hotel, what time rehearsal is, whether you are to play alto or tenor sax—or both—how much you'll be paid for overtime, who authorizes overtime, and on and on.

Often small details make a job successful, and this aspect of the music business should not be treated lightly. Your agent is a go-between for you and the client, and you must pay close attention to be sure that all the details are covered, understood, and agreed upon. Try to have a contract or a written letter confirming these important points.

• You may need to use your musical expertise to advise agents. Sometimes, in the heat of a sales call, an agent will promise the moon, but *you* will be on the hot seat if you can't deliver. Don't let an agent sell your five-piece rock band as a jazz ensemble or your sixteen-piece big band as a top-forty group.

• *Never ever* try to "steal" a client from an agent. When you play a job that an agent has booked, you should refer any inquiries generated by that job to the agent. Never hand out your own card at an agent-booked job; carry a few cards from the agency. Good agents work very hard to find and book jobs, and you'll quickly find yourself blacklisted if you try to go around them to book yourself direct with their clients.

(This does not mean that you shouldn't try to book yourself when no written or implied agreement with an agent is compromised. Just don't try to steal clients who "belong" to your agent.)

• Always have a clear understanding with the agency about money. Is the price quoted net to you or does the agency's commission come out of it? Will the client pay the agent direct, or should you pick up a check? Will the agent pay you immediately following the job, or will you have to wait weeks or even months until the agent has been paid by the client? If the worst happens and the client doesn't pay, will the agent pay you anyway? Or if the job is canceled two days before the performance, will you be paid?

Misunderstandings about money have ruined many relationships between musicians and booking agents. If you have a firm, clear— better yet, *written*—understanding about these matters with your agent, you'll both be happier and more prosperous.

LOVE-HATE IS HERE TO STAY

Usually, the basis for tension between musicians and their agents is that they are trying to do very different things. At the simplest level, the difference in what the agent wants and what the musician wants cannot be reconciled. The best you can do is understand it and know where your agent's loyalty lies.

Musicians want to play, to play as well as they can, and to derive as much personal satisfaction as they can from their performances. Perhaps making money is part of the goal, but it's not always first on the list. Many musicians' allegiance is, essentially, to their music, their art, and their craft.

Agents, on the other hand, are businesspeople whose loyalty is with their hard-earned clients. Their principal interest is in maintaining those clients and their business. When there is a musician-client conflict, the agent will *automatically* take the client's side, right or wrong. Why? Because that's where the money comes from. Musicians can easily be replaced, but if a client goes to another agency that account, and its revenue, is lost.

By accepting the reality of this basic difference in orientation, you'll save yourself a lot of misapprehension and unpleasantness. Regardless of what they tell you, agents represent their paying clients—not you, unless you're a star or celebrity—and their aim is to keep those clients satisfied. Don't be shocked, That's their job.

So, at a convention where you're providing walk-up and awards music before playing the show, don't be surprised if the agent—on behalf of the client—asks you not to take a break but to play two and a half hours straight. If that's what the client wants, that's what the agent wants.

All this doesn't mean, of course, that agents are your enemies. It's just that if you understand what the bottom line really is, you can avoid needless conflict and make your relationship more productive.

IT TAKES MONEY TO MAKE MONEY

Why are agents entitled to part of your money? Simply because they've earned it, doing things that you may not know how to do or may dislike doing. Besides, a good agent is an expert salesperson and can probably sell your talents better than you can.

There are various reasons that an agent should—in fact, *must*— get a percentage of the total.

If your agent, Mark Smithers, has an office, then his overhead is much higher than yours. He has to pay substantial rent and utilities. His ad in the Yellow Pages may cost several hundred dollars a year. The installation cost for a business phone is two to three times that of a home phone, and the monthly charges are much higher. Nobody gives him letterheads, envelopes, invoices, typewriters, adding machines, computers, gasoline, business lunches, membership in the convention bureau (which may cost one or two thousand dollars), or his business insurance. His office copy machine probably cost him two thousand dollars.

If Mark has a staff, his bookkeeping load is enormous, with federal, state, and local regulations to comply with and licenses and taxes to pay. He must hire a bookkeeper to compute withholding, unemployment, and workers' compensation. He must hire a secretary to type letters proposing your services to clients. He must hire, and probably train, salespeople to sell your musical services to clients.

And Mark may spend a hundred dollars in long-distance phone bills, business lunches, and postage trying to book your group for a job, only to lose the business to a competitor who quoted a slightly lower price. In short, it may cost even a small agency *five or six thousand dollars a month* just to keep the office running.

The cost of doing business is high, and your agent, who finds work for you, deserves the percentage that he gets. Thank him. Don't begrudge him his fee. Much of the work Mark finds for you is work you'd never otherwise get, so you are gaining, not losing by using his services.

Unfortunately, there are shady agents. Usually, their poor reputations will warn you to be careful. Stay away from the ones who don't pay promptly or don't pay the agreed-upon amount. Avoid those whose jobs cancel frequently or who don't abide by standard agreements. One bad experience with a booking agency should warn you to watch your step. Two such experiences should end your relationship. Most booking agents, however, especially the established ones who prosper, are hardworking and honest businesspeople who need your music as much as you need their sales talent.

LONG-TERM AGREEMENTS

What should you do if Mark, your agent, wants you to sign an exclusive contract so that all your performances and self-promotions must be booked through him? For most freelance musicians, this situation won't arise, but possibly an agent or producer will promise lots of money if you will "sign an exclusive."

Find a lawyer with experience in entertainment. *Never* sign a long-term contract with an agent, producer, or recording company without having *your* attorney check it over.

It may be that an exclusive agreement would, in fact, be a great thing for you and for the agency. But it might be a very bad idea, because if you have no way out of a one-sided contract, you could be out of luck.

If an agent wants to be your exclusive representative, you must know if you are *guaranteed* a certain amount of work, or money, or publicity. Don't sign a contract on the basis of good intentions, excellent prospects, or even years of friendship. With your lawyer's help, consider:

- *Does the exclusive contract require the agent to book you a certain number of jobs for a specified rate of pay? Or does it just require him to try?*
- *What if your old college roommate wants you to play for her wedding, free? Would your exclusive contract force you to pay the agency a commission on your own gift to a friend?*
- *What if your record doesn't sell as well as expected? Is the producer or record company still obligated to spend a certain amount of money and effort on publicity and advertising?*
- *What if you break your arm and can't play the planned series of concerts? Could you be liable for your agent's lost profits?*
- *What if the planned series of concerts fizzles out? Will you be released from the contract if the promoter fails to deliver the promised crowds?*
- *What if clients approach you directly? Will you be obligated to pay a commission to the agency from your profits? This is not an uncommon problem for freelance players, but careful planning will help you avoid it.*

These are a few of the kinds of questions that should be *legally* settled, *to your lawyer's satisfaction,* before you sign any long-term agreement. It's not that you should mistrust those who show an interest in your career. It's just that agents, producers, promoters, and record companies are primarily looking out for themselves. That is not the same thing as looking out for you. You'll have to do that yourself.

GOOD TEAMWORK CAN PAY OFF

Establishing a good relationship with all the appropriate agents in your area can be an excellent first step for you. You need to work a lot of jobs, and the professional sales staff of a dynamic agency can help you meet your goal. As your musical life expands, be sure to keep these agencies updated about your new abilities, repertory, and equipment. They need to know what you have to sell.

Don't ignore the national agencies like Ray Bloch, Jack Morton, and Alkahest. Even if they don't have offices in your community, they may occasionally need to provide music for a client in your town. Put them on your brochure mailing list so that when they need your kind of talent in your area they'll know whom to call.

The teamwork between a good musician and a good agent can be very productive, with each person doing what he or she knows (and likes) best. When you work through an honest, hardworking agency you'll find that music and business aren't incompatible after all.

15

Selling

Must you—yourself—sell your music?

Yes. You won't make any money until someone—a client, an agent, or another musician—pays you to play. You must convince someone to hire you, and that's selling.

You may protest that you're a musician and not a salesperson, but selling is not as difficult or intimidating as you probably think. You have focused your PMMS on people who are apt to pay for your kind of music, so now you have to let them know what you can do.

You should think of selling your music as an information service to potential clients. You're informing them that the music they *need* is available . . . from you.

IF YOU DON'T TELL THEM, WHO WILL?

Maybe your mother taught you humility. That's a good trait, but not when it comes to selling your music. Now you need to be a little aggressive—not high-pressure, though, and certainly not obnoxious. You'll have to learn to talk about yourself and the merits of your music.

Bear in mind that there are more musicians looking than there are jobs available and that your competitors may be out there calling on *your* potential clients. There's only one thing to do—sell your talents. Let people know what you can do.

You'll have an edge over other kinds of salespeople, for you'll be touting yourself and your music. Who knows your abilities better than you? If you know, absolutely, that you can do the job, you'll demonstrate the confidence that will help you sell.

Your Public-Relations Tools

To do an effective job of selling your music, you should be prepared with a few well-produced printed aids. These need not be expensive. If you're artistically inclined, you can design them yourself and have them reproduced at a local quick-copy center.

Shun the stock illustrations your printer has on hand. Instead, commission a commercial artist to design a logo or illustration for your card and other stationery. Some commercial art students do excellent work at low prices, but be sure to look at samples of similar work. Avoid clutter. Aim for a simple, memorable design. Almost everything about music is graphically interesting, and a good artist can use such elements as the staff, notes, keyboard, or instrument shapes to develop a design that you will use for years. And it will be yours alone. Here are the PR tools you'll need.

Business cards. Every musician must have business cards. Since these represent you to potential clients, be sure your cards are well done. Use good-quality stock, a clearly legible typeface, and a simple design that matches your style.

You should have a separate card for different facets of your music; one for teaching, one for your band, and a different card entirely for your solo concert work. Trite phrases such as "Music for all occasions" probably won't help and might even harm.

Joe Girard, the "world's greatest salesman" (see Appendix B), throws handfuls of his cards into the air at football games. Although you probably won't need to be quite *that* enterprising, you'll want everyone who could need your music to have a card. Always carry a good supply. Many businesspeople keep business-card files, so clip a card to all your correspondence.

Brochures, flyers, information sheets. Most freelancers need at least one brochure, folder, or information sheet. These can be as simple as a single piece of paper with a *neatly typed* description of what you can do. Be sure your *grammar, usage, and spelling* are correct; mistakes can be distracting and look unprofessional. An offset printer can turn your clean, camera-ready copy into inexpensive but useful publicity pieces. Your printer can show you how a single sheet can be folded to form a brochure or flyer, and he or she will gladly refer you to artists and typesetters if you need them. (See Appendix F.)

Your printed aids should simply tell:

- *Who you are.*
- *What you do.*
- *Where you have worked and for whom.*
- *How your music will enhance specific kinds of events.*
- *What others have said about your work. Keep copies of good reviews and letters and use them in preparing dynamic sales aids.*

Be positive and creative, but stick to the truth. If you've never been to Las Vegas, don't bill yourself as "just back from Vegas." Lies can lead to big trouble.

Photographs. All musicians should have a supply of good, *up-to-date eight-by-ten-inch photos.* Black-and-white pictures are usually fine; color costs a lot more. Get a good photo and use a duplication house (see Appendix C) to make copies and add your name at the bottom.

Audio/video tapes. Some musicians will profit from the use of audio or video demonstration tapes. If you record your music, make sure that the tapes are representative of your talent and appropriate to the client's needs. Make sure, too, that they are very well produced.

Almost everyone has a good sound system at home or at the office—maybe one in the car. Your potential client, through media exposure, has been trained to expect professional-sounding music, even in soap commercials. Be positive that your tape at least approaches this quality. In other words, don't make demo tapes with a thirty-dollar cassette player and a built-in microphone.

FEATURE YOURSELF

Newspaper, magazine, and radio and television writers in your area, believe it or not, are on constant lookout for interesting material for feature stories. You should try to get valuable publicity for yourself or your group by letting them know anything unusual about your musical activities. Writers on daily papers and reporters for local TV news shows have to fill their space or time every day, so if you're doing something out of the ordinary with your music—and you should be—you should let them know about it.

Think creatively. Is what you are doing—or are about to do—good story material? What's the attention grabber? Does it have broad appeal? Is it interesting—to nonmusicians? Pass your ideas to the entertainment or feature editors in your area.

Why do you need publicity? You are building a career in an increasingly competitive profession, and your name should—really *must*—become widely known. When people think of the most outstanding piano teacher, dance band, or folk singer in your community, they should think of *you*. Continuing publicity is part of building name recognition. Think of publicity as free advertising and always be aware of how your musical activities could interest others. Here are a few ideas for feature stories:

- *Announcements of recitals, concerts, or musical programs can be turned into feature stories if something uncommon or special is included. You might, say, relate your graduation recital to your town's history by performing the work of a local composer. Perhaps your high school band has been judged "superior" at the last ten band festivals, and you are trying for a record-breaking eleventh. Advise the feature writers in your area, and also notify all the compilers of the events calendars that appear in newspapers and on radio and TV.*

- *Have you played for so many high-society dances and debutante balls that you've become an indispensable part of the social scene? A profile about you in a regional magazine could make interesting reading—and create valuable publicity for you.*

- *Reviews in newspaper entertainment sections offer another way for you to let the public know what you are doing. Often these reviews cover all the entertainment in an area, so let editorial reviewers know where you are performing and ask to be reviewed. It will help if you provide good quality, black-and-white photos to be run with any reviews.*

- *Anything unusual or especially noteworthy can be material for a news or feature story. Are you trying to get in the* Guinness Book of World Records *by playing the accordion nonstop for two weeks? Did you narrowly escape death when you forgot to check the polarity on your amplifiers and were severely shocked at an outdoor concert? Have you organized a fund-raising event for hungry people in your community? Have you played the piano in the same hotel lounge for twenty-five years? Did you accidentally drop your Steinberger bass from a six-story balcony— but not even knock it out of tune? Do you have an impressive collection of antique wind instruments?*

So, think creatively and present your ideas in such a way that the writer or editor you approach will see the broad appeal of your ideas. Don't forget that writers and editors *need* stories every day, week, or month. Help them find interesting material by telling them about your musical achievements and music-related experiences.

Once a story has appeared about you and your music, be sure that you use it to further your career. You can add impressive quotations to your publicity material or enclose photocopies of the story with your brochure when you do mailings. See Appendix B for further reading on creating publicity.

If a TV piece has been done on you, be sure to get a videotape copy, and let prospective clients know of its availability.

SALES BASICS FOR MUSICIANS

There are many excellent books on salesmanship. Visit your library or bookstore and read a few of those listed in Appendix B. It will be worth your while to learn from master salespeople. The following basic principles, however, will get you started.

Plan your approach. Before your first sales call to a prospective client, think in detail about what you have to offer. Know *exactly* what you want to sell, what you can do, and how much you expect to be paid. Work on variations of your basic idea and write these ideas down and review them until you know them well. Many salespeople write such information on three-by-five-inch index cards. They arrange and re-arrange the cards to get the best sequence for each presentation.

Practice your sales pitch on your spouse or friends. Have them ask you hard questions. The client will.

If you know in advance what kind of music the client will need, write out a specific proposal before your sales call. Leave a copy with the prospect and, needless to say, keep a copy for your files. Specify what you are offering, for how long, and how much it will cost.

Make an appointment. Never drop in on a prospect. Assume that your potential clients are busy and that their time is valuable. You must follow standard business practices when dealing with business-people, so call ahead for an appointment.

Ask for your prospect by name whenever possible. If you know only the company name, use your experience and common sense to reach the music buyer. If you are calling on a hotel, for example, you'll probably need the catering or sales department. In a large corporation, you'll deal with the public-relations, meeting-planning, or protocol staff.

If you know the event you'd like to talk about, simply ask the operator to connect you with the person in charge of that project, whether it's a Christmas party or an annual company meeting. With good telephone manners and friendly persistence you can usually reach the right person. Get the proper spelling of your contact's name, and note whether it's "Miss," "Mrs.," or "Ms."

Be punctual. When you have an appointment, be on time or a few minutes early. Whatever you do, don't be late. Allow for rush-hour traffic and parking problems.

Many businesspeople are suspicious of musicians and artists. When you call on them, you must show that you can abide by their rules. Punctuality is crucial. Why should a client believe that your band will start on time if you're late for your initial meeting?

Be appropriately dressed. Use your client's style as a guide. Don't flaunt your independence from business conventions by dressing too casually; it will set the wrong tone for your meeting.

Be neat and clean. It may seem like stating the obvious, but clean nails, neat hair, and fresh breath are important.

Talk about your prospect's music needs. Ask questions and really listen to the answers.

Try to avoid the word *I* as much as possible. Emphasize *you* because that's what your client is ultimately interested in—what he wants, what you can do for him. (Your prospective client, of course, could as likely be a woman.)

Assess what kind of music is needed and make suggestions that would fulfill these requirements. Show him, in detail, how your music will do what he wants. Emphasize that you'll make him look good to his boss.

Be honest. If a prospect needs something that you can't provide, you'd best tell him so. Never book a job you can't perform well just because you need the money. Both you and your client will lose, and bad news travels fast.

Use backup material. Give him your brochure. Show him your videotape. Tell him about other clients you've successfully worked for. Give him references (but be sure they're willing to be called on as such). Let him read a few good thank you letters from satisfied clients.

State your price. Tell him confidently, not apologetically, what you charge. To speak with self-assurance in stating your price, you must determine beforehand the monetary worth of the job you are proposing and be prepared to fill out a contract form. Don't be timid. Be ready to talk about money—that's what businesspeople deal with every day. (The next chapter goes into detail about pricing your services and preparing contracts.)

Take the initiative. When you've told him what you can do for him, ask for a commitment. Don't be vague or wishy-washy. Don't be embarrassed to talk about money; he knows music isn't free.

If you know you can provide what he needs, take out a contract form and say, "Now, shall we get the specifics down in writing so I can hold this date for you?"

Don't prolong the meeting. When you've finished your presentation, leave. No further sales pitch is wanted after you've gotten a "yes," "no," or "not at this time." Don't overstay your welcome and don't be *too* aggressive. A good relationship can be more valuable than any single sale.

FOLLOW UP

Write it down. Immediately after leaving a prospect's office, write down all the important details you discussed. *Don't trust your memory.* If you need to contact the client or prospect in the future, write a reminder on your calendar or put one in your tickler file.

Send a note of appreciation. Write a short thank-you note to each prospect you see, whether he buys music from you or not. If he bought, send a contract with the note. If he didn't, write the note anyway. He'll have a more positive impression if you show your appreciation.

Continue to follow up. Keep in touch with potential clients whether they are businesspeople, agents, or other musicians. Buyers get in ruts, too, and you need to remind them of your availability.

But don't be a pest. An occasional phone call, mailed brochure, or short sales call will keep your name before good prospects. Easy, but regular, does it.

PEOPLE NEED MUSIC

Remember that *every* client is concerned with his or her needs. We all are self-centered, and your clients aren't necessarily altruists. They want their money's worth.

People don't *require* music the way they need food or shelter, so keep in mind that you are selling a luxury. Thus, you must emphasize what your music can do for prospective clients and show how it will help them in some way. Appeal to their egos and pride as well as their other reasons for buying good music.

Be ready to prove to your potential clients that not only do they need music—they need *your* music. Practice making your selling points in advance so that your sales calls will be enthusiastic and convincing. Here are a few ideas about what music can do. You'll think of more.

Music creates an appropriate atmosphere. Music can be sophisticated, exciting, sedate, lively, contemporary, country, ethnic, celebratory, cultured—you name it. It can set the pace of an event and establish the tone of a gathering.

Live music demonstrates affluence. If your client can afford to have a dance band at a garden party, the guests will be impressed. Sometimes music is a status symbol.

Music makes an event memorable. For a wedding reception, sales meeting, cocktail function, grand opening, or whatever, music can turn an ordinary party into a happening. The photographs of Uncle Albert dancing with all the young girls will be family treasures for years.

Music entertains. The right soloist or group will turn another routine company dinner into a great evening.

Music breaks the ice, encourages mixing, mingling, and talking. If your client's salespeople are dancing with potential customers in a hospitality suite, you can bet you have a happy client.

Music brings people together by bridging cultural, generational, and background differences.

Music sells. Television jingles may cost tens of thousands of dollars to produce—for only thirty or sixty seconds of music. Why pay that much? Because memorable melodies sell.

Music inspires. Pep bands at football games do it; so can you.

Music makes people feel good. If your clients and their guests end up doing the twist, they're probably happy.

Music attracts crowds. A dixieland band in a shopping mall quickly creates a sensation.

Music recalls nostalgic memories. It recreates times past. Your clients will enjoy saying, "They played that when I was in college."

Music helps and heals. Therapists know that music has powers to soothe and calm.

Music even helps people fall in love.

CLIENTS NEED YOUR MUSIC

Even after you convince your prospect that music is essential, your work still isn't over. You've got to convince him or her to hire *you*. Once again, be prepared with as many persuasive reasons as possible why your group is exactly what is needed.

Use the Personal Sales Ideas Worksheet at the end of this chapter to collect your own best selling points. Here are a few suggestions. You should think of more that fit your particular situation, and know them so well that you can answer any objection.

- *You're professional. This is what you do for a living and you provide better quality than part-timers can produce.*

- *Or, if you're a part-time player, you could argue that you aren't a jaded, bored professional. Point out that you play because you love music and that your enthusiasm and energy will make up for any lack of professional expertise.*

- *Repeat that you understand the client's needs well and can provide exactly that kind of music. Give examples to prove your point.*

- *Remind the prospect that you've played dozens, or hundreds, of similar engagements. You might even say something like, "I'll bet your boss will love us."*

- *Explain that your equipment is the best and that the quality of your music is therefore better than the competition's. Offer to let the client use your state-of-the-art sound system for speeches, toasts, or whatever, thus saving the cost of renting another public-address unit.*

- *Underline that your band will be not just on time, but early. Tell the client that you will set up your equipment before the party if necessary.*

- *Show how low your price really is when divided by the number of guests or in comparison with the total price of the event. Sometimes a wedding cake costs as much as a small combo—even though the band is much more important to the success of the reception.*

- *If the job you're going after requires virtuosity, expound on your virtuosity—if you possess it. If variety is the key, explain that you* can play the full spectrum that will be needed—if you can. (Don't exaggerate your abilities. If you don't perform up to expectations, you will be on the hot seat—and will lose the client.)

- *If you can, present letters of commendation resulting from similar jobs and offer a list of current and former clients that you know will vouch for your music. Again, word of mouth has very strong persuasive power.*

If you prepare and make well-thought-out sales presentations, your prospects will realize that you can, indeed, help them. Then they will no longer be prospects. They will be clients.

PERSONAL SALES IDEAS WORKSHEET

What My Music Can Do ———————————————

What's Best about My Music ———————————————

What Others Have Liked about My Music ———————————

Why My Music Is a Bargain ———————————————

Why I'm Better than My Competition ————————————

16

Pricing and Contracts

As you locate clients who are willing to pay you to perform, it's essential that you know how much your music is worth to them—and also to you.

Then, once price and other details have been settled, you need to send contracts or letters of confirmation.

These details are sometimes tiresome, even boring. But they are crucial nonetheless.

HOW MUCH SHOULD YOU CHARGE?
HOW MUCH ARE YOU WORTH?

Make the price right. Try to price your music just above the average for your community. If you quote too low, your client will be suspi-

155

cious and won't respect you. And your colleagues will be hostile if they learn that you undershoot the norm. If you price yourself too high, however, you'll lose sales.

How do you know what to charge for your music? This is a difficult question, and you'll find that there will be a good bit of variation as you sell.

Find out what your competitors charge by calling them (or having a friend do it) and getting their price for a particular kind of job. Keep a list of what other musicians and agents request for certain musical services. Remember, too, that many variables influence the price; you'll charge more in December than in July, more on Saturday night than Tuesday afternoon, more for driving sixty miles than driving six blocks, more if equipment must be carried up two flights of steps, and more to General Motors than to a bride's father.

Know, ultimately, what it's worth to you, and stick to it. If the going price for a three-hour solo piano job in your area is $200, know in advance whether you'd play it for $150. Or $100. You'll need to be flexible, but it's very important to stick to your standards. Business clients expect it; they wouldn't sell their services at half price and neither should you.

If you have an exclusive, a really special act, you should obviously ask for more money.

Remember that many large companies expect to spend lots of money. Think in their terms, not yours.

If you have to cut your price, try to cut your proposal a corresponding amount. That is, you could drop an instrument or cut an hour from the total to justify a price reduction.

Here are more suggestions for pricing your music.

Join a union, if one is active in your area. In many parts of the country the American Federation of Musicians is involved in all aspects of professional music, and membership offers several advantages. One is *union scale,* which should be your *minimum* charge. Usually, scale is a complex system of charges, based on the kind of job involved, the purpose of the music, length of job, number of musicians, and so on. Sometimes, scale is too low for your talent and your market. In that case, raise your price. Other times scale will keep the price up, and you'll be glad you're affiliated with the union.

When you get involved in recording work—jingles, demos, industrial film scores, for example—you'll find that union scale can be very important. A union may keep close watch on studios and recording clients, and often residual payments continue to come in long after the recording is finished. These are payments that the client makes each time your recorded music is used. In such cases, payment is fixed by the union, and its rules and regulations must be strictly followed.

For other kinds of music—top-forty lounge work, for instance—you may find that the union is not involved in your area. Nevertheless, if you know what the scale is for your kind of job, you'll have a starting point for deciding how much to charge. Union addresses are included in Appendix D.

Remember that agency profits and expenses must be added to your fees; you may decide to take a little less when booking through an agency. In return, however, you should expect the agency to take care of such business details as contracts and billing.

On the other hand, when you book directly, your price should be competitive with agency charges. In other words, don't undercut the agents, or they'll quit using you.

Never perform free of charge unless it is for a very good cause and you are philanthropically contributing your time and talent. Only amateurs play "for exposure," and such exposure is almost always nonexistent and thus worthless. If you play without a fee, you are likely to be taken advantage of.

If you are asked to contribute your time and music to a legitimate charity or fund-raising event, think carefully before you donate your music. It's likely that other participants are being paid—the caterer, florist, and photographer, for example—and you should be no different. Often legitimate fund-raising events have considerable production budgets, and the money is raised from those who pay to attend, not from those who perform. If you do perform gratis, you should get a letter from the sponsor thanking you for your specific donation so that you can at least claim a tax deduction.

This is not an unfriendly, unfeeling approach to charities. There are so many good causes that you could give your music away every day. Unfortunately, that won't help pay the rent.

Make a chart listing all your prices for various sized groups and different kinds of jobs. Then you'll be able to quote prices promptly when talking to different clients. Devising such a chart isn't easy because you need to be consistent and fair to yourself while not charging too much or too little. Should a three-hour job cost the client three times as much as a one-hour job? Should overtime simply be prorated, or should your overtime rate be a little higher to compensate for unexpected changes in your schedule?

Incidentally, you'll probably discover that the more you charge, the more you are respected. Interestingly, the opposite is usually true, too. The less you charge, the poorer your reputation—not to mention your pocketbook.

Don't forget to include any extras the union or "local custom" adds. There probably is a standard extra fee for rehearsal time and for shows. But what about cartage for heavy, hard-to-move instruments such as pianos, drum sets, harps, and organs?

Often, too, you must add "doubling fees" for players who provide and play more than one instrument. In some cities, doubles add 25 percent per instrument, and a reed player who doubles on flute, clarinet, and two or three different saxes will make considerably more money than the trombone player who plays only his or her primary instrument. These factors are very important in large cities and on large jobs. Make sure that *all* the important fees are included when you quote a price.

Television and videotaping have other, usually higher, scales and sometimes present pitfalls to unwary musicians. More than one band (usually in large, very union-conscious cities) has walked out when the client started videotaping a stage show or business meeting without paying "video production scale." Be sure you and your musicians will be paid for your music if the client decides to make a training film or videotape of your performance. And be sure this is understood in advance.

One Atlanta singer, making a videotape for her own sales use, was stunned that the twelve-piece band backing her show insisted on an extra payment of over $50 per player to permit her to videotape the proceedings. She had thought the musicians would be happy to help her produce a videotape that would sell the show *and* their backup music. The band members, however, didn't agree, and they refused to play without assurances that video scale would be paid for the job.

Charge what the market will bear. As you work more, and are more and more in demand, you'll probably want to follow the basic free-market pricing strategy and charge what you can get. One local four-piece group specializing in Jewish music recently raised its price from $600 to $900 per three-hour job without losing any clients. If you are the best, or only, show in town, you may be able to raise your price accordingly. Be careful, however, not to disregard your community's norms, or you may price yourself out of the market. And obviously, when you charge more, you should provide more variety and better-quality and entertainment for the client's dollar.

GET IT IN WRITING

Once you and your client have agreed on the details of the job and you have been hired, it's time to send a contract. There are two very important reasons why you should *always have a contract or letter of confirmation:*

1. Writing down the details in black and white reduces the chances for a misunderstanding. Spell out the time of day and the date. There is always room for error, but if you have a signed contract hiring you for seven o'clock on Tuesday, May 12, your client can't claim that you should have been there at six o'clock on Monday, May 11. This is not a far-fetched example; such mistakes happen every day.

2. If the worst should happen, and your client won't pay you, a signed contract will be crucial when you go to the union, or to court, to claim your money.

WHAT SHOULD A CONTRACT INCLUDE?

What form should your contract take? What points should it cover? This book does not offer legal advice, and if you need an ironclad contract you should probably consult an attorney. However, for most situations, that won't be necessary, and clarity is what you're after. Here are some considerations:

• If you are in a musician's union, usually the American Federation of Musicians, use its standard contract form. It is widely recognized, covers the important points clearly, and protects you as much as possible.

- If you aren't a union member or if you'd prefer to devise your own contract or confirmation letter, be sure that it includes all the necessary information. Standard practice is to send two signed copies to the client—one for him or her, and one to be returned, signed, to you. Sometimes a third copy is required for the union.

One good idea is to have your own contract form printed on your letterhead and include clauses pertinent to you. This personalizes the contract, makes you seem more professional, and saves you time. If you decide to create your own standard form, be sure to include:

- *Today's date*
- *Name, address, telephone number, and title of the client*
- *Definition of the band or group—size and instrumentation*
- *Compensation agreed on, and when payment will be made*
- *Overtime charges, if necessary*
- *Deposit required, if any, and conditions for refunding it*
- *Appropriate dress for the job*
- *Special requirements or requests*

In addition, you may wish to include preprinted "conditions" clauses that will be applicable to all your jobs. Unexpected circumstances can cause real problems, and you'll avoid confusion if you decide, *in advance,* what to do. Here are a few ideas you may find useful.

- What if the affair is canceled? The wedding is called off, there's a death in the family, or the couple starts divorce proceedings a week before their anniversary party. Will you return the deposit, or is it (as it usually is) nonrefundable?

- What if bad weather causes a last-minute change? Snowstorms, ice storms, tornadoes, and hurricanes can play havoc with plans. If extremely bad weather is remotely possible in your area, make provisions for it in your contract.

- What if a sudden rainstorm forces the garden party to move indoors with only one hour remaining? You may wish to add an extra setup fee or cartage charge to compensate for the unpleasant task of moving unexpectedly during a job.

Or perhaps the client just forgot to tell you that the cocktail hour will be by the pool, the dinner will be up two flights of stairs on the deck, and the dance will be in the ballroom. If you've written in an extra fee for any location moves, you'll feel better as you drag your set of drums up and down all those steps.

• If the client is providing an instrument for you to play—usually a piano—specify that it be in reasonable tune and in good working order. Or require that it must be tuned prior to your performance. Add a cartage fee for bringing your own equipment to the job in case theirs isn't playable when you arrive.

• You may wish to add an extra fee for early setup time or a consulting fee for extra meetings with the clients. What if the host of a house party wants you to drive forty miles out to "look over" the room where you'll be playing? Will you charge for the extra trip? What if the bride and groom want to have a two-hour meeting to discuss the music for their two-hour reception? Will you charge for your time?

• What if you have to buy special music and spend time transposing and learning it for a wedding ceremony? You may have to buy a twelve-dollar book you'll never use again to find one obscure tune. Will you pass this charge on to the client?

If you simply spell out these items as stipulations in your standard contract form and note that they apply to all jobs, you'll save many headaches and much confusion. Usually, just deciding in advance what to do will ensure that the engagement goes smoothly.

Maybe your kind of music doesn't require so much detail, or maybe you don't work that many jobs. In these cases, a simple letter to your client will probably suffice, but be sure to include any pertinent details mentioned above. Use your letterhead and be simple and direct. Here's an example:

September 17, 1985

Mr. John Class, Manager
Proper Country Club
Lake Superior, New York

Dear Mr. Class:

This letter will confirm our engagement to provide music for your special "Autumn Days" party to be held on Saturday, October 12, 1985, from nine o'clock until midnight in your club's main ballroom. My band, "The Mellowtones," consists of five pieces plus a female vocalist, and will be dressed formally.

As we discussed on the phone, we will provide our own sound system but will use the house piano. You have assured me that the piano will be in good tune and placed on the stage by seven o'clock that evening.

Our fee for this engagement is $900, to be paid to me at the end of the evening. If overtime is required the rate is $150 per *half hour.*

We will, as usual, begin the evening by playing the club's theme song, "Give Me the Simple Life." If there are other special requests, please let me know in advance.

One copy of this letter is for your file, and the second copy should be signed and returned to me.

Thanks again for all your help. We are looking forward to another fine engagement at the Proper Country Club.

Sincerely,

Joe Jones,
Bandleader

Accepted by _____

(Address)

_____

(Telephone)

_____

Obviously, you'd save time by using a standard contract form and not having to write a complete letter to each client. Also, if you use a form, you won't be as likely to overlook any important points.

In any case, whether you have an attorney help you devise an ironclad contract or just write a confirmation letter like the sample included here, be sure you get a written agreement. Everything will go better if you do, and you might be sorry if you don't.

17

Playing the Job

Now you've booked a job—or dozens of them. The hardest part of the freelance music business, finding work, is behind you. Your next concern is that the job itself goes well.

For one thing, you'd like to work again for this client. For another, your reputation as "the musician to call" is built one job at a time. What makes a memorable job and a happy client? What makes a job go over well?

Part of the answer has little to do with music. In fact, *the success of a job often depends on nonmusical factors.* It's not just how (or what) you play. It may be whether your shoes are shined or whether you start on time. Little things mean a lot, and the values of the business world don't parallel those of many musicians.

DO'S AND DON'TS FOR EVERY JOB

Here are some recommendations that apply to all freelance music jobs. While they won't guarantee success, they'll get you started.

Know what you're supposed to do. This isn't as easy as it sounds. Be sure you understand what the client wants. When she says she wants classical music, does she mean Beethoven or Cole Porter? Or does she think classical music is anything soft and slow and written before 1950? Some clients are musically naive, so be careful to define terms.

Vagueness always causes trouble. If your client wants jazz, that could mean swing or fusion, Louis Armstrong or Wynton Marsalis. Clear communication and definition of terms solve this problem. It can be helpful to get specific suggestions from the client to find out what he really has in mind.

Try to determine the client's *intangible* and *indefinite* needs. Is he trying to hire a band that will please his boss? Is he trying to impress his guests with his sophistication? Or does he want a rowdy, good-time atmosphere? If you can accurately assess your client's needs, *stated or not,* you'll have a much better chance of fulfilling them.

Communicate during the job. Check periodically with your client to be sure that everything is going well. Sometimes she won't complain until it's too late, or for some reason she may feel awkward about interrupting your performance to request a change.

Your selection of tunes, stage demeanor, volume, lighting, tempo, and so on can be changed if necessary. Remember, in commercial situations you're hired to fulfill a particular need, not necessarily to express yourself musically.

A cliché is appropriate here: The boss may not always be right, but he's always the boss. If your client wants to hear "New York, New York" again (for the fifth time), play it again. Grit your teeth and bear it, think about the money you'll make from that tune, or play it in a different key for practice.

Try to avoid the musician-client hostility that sometimes develops. The easiest way to keep everyone happy is to keep talking. Communicate with your client.

Details are crucial. To repeat, the quality of the music doesn't always determine the success of a job. Often it's the little things, the insignificant details so easy to overlook, that the client will remember.

So be early to the job. Check the lighting, the sound, the piano, the location of the service elevator, parking, whether the electrical outlets work, where you can store your equipment cases, and where the dressing rooms are.

Make sure that the house lights won't be turned off just when you start reading the most important music of the evening, and be certain that turning off the house lights won't also turn off your electricity.

Find out if the musicians are invited to eat and drink with the guests, who authorizes overtime, what the boss's favorite song is, what the newlyweds' first dance will be.

Don't forget to double-check with musicians you have hired about time, place, instruments needed, doubles, rehearsals, proper dress, and pay. Remember to have extra music-stand light bulbs, guitar cords, bow ties, and whatever else is most likely to break or be forgotten.

It is unfortunate, but even though your music is perfectly chosen and performed, the client may remember only that you started ten minutes late or that the sax player wore a blue shirt instead of white.

The music must be right and as good as possible, but don't overlook all those little, but important, details.

Keep it all under control. When you are asked to do the impossible, don't be hostile. The client, or audience, probably doesn't understand the technical reasons why your trio can't sound like Michael Jackson's latest hit. Don't try to explain by talking about overdubs, studio musicians, backup singers, and so on; the client will probably think you are just making excuses. It's easier to explain politely that you don't know the requested song and suggest something similar that you *can* do. Nobody knows everything (except teenaged audiences).

One way to stay in control is to have the next tune always in mind. Wasting time between numbers will make your audience restless and give people time to think up hundreds of requests that you can't do.

Always tune instruments, replace broken strings, and test microphones *before* the job begins. Nothing is as irritating to people enjoying a quiet dinner, for example, as loud guitar tuning or repeated "Testing, 1, 2, 3 . . ." Of course tuning and testing are crucial, but do them early, before the job begins.

Follow up. Write a short thank-you note to the client after the job (unless it was booked through an agency). Let her know that you appreciate her business and that you'd like to work with her again. Enclose your card. If you're sending an invoice, a thank-you note will soften its impact. In any case, the extra few minutes spent following up will be appreciated.

Your client has no doubt paid you a considerable sum of money. Don't vanish without a trace. You'll need her again.

Maintain enthusiasm. A professional level of competence is certainly important to your success as a freelance musician, but so is your attitude, your demeanor while playing for money. There are lots of excellent musicians who barely make a living, while many less-proficient players make much more money. Why should this be so?

If you regard playing music commercially as a chore, your attitude will inevitably be communicated to your listeners, and they'll resent it. If you're taking their money, they can rightly expect your cheerful best.

If you're bored with a particular job or tired, don't show it. Try to show enthusiasm instead. This can be hard to do, but it's worth the effort.

Consider yourself fortunate, as a freelance musician, to be paid for doing what you most enjoy. Play each job as though you welcome the opportunity. You might make more money in another profession, but you'd miss the excitement and the joy of music.

18

The Successful Freelance Musician

Some freelance musicians always seem to do well, constantly working and in demand. Other, perhaps more talented, players sit at home and watch TV. What determines success? How can you continue to expand the demand for your music? Here are some suggestions.

PRACTICE, PRACTICE, PRACTICE!

Like a doctor or lawyer, musicians *practice* their profession. You'll never know everything about music, and you'll never reach perfection. But you'll certainly be better off by working at it.

One way to keep yourself fresh and ensure demand for your music is to continue to practice. Learn new tunes, master current styles.

Try not to become so identified with one type of music that your career depends on its continued popularity. You probably won't like every new musical fad, but if you understand and can play the "latest" well, you'll be in a better position to market your skills. That's because you'll have more skills to market.

Playing music is like athletic ability: use it or lose it. Practice is the way to win in the freelance music competition . . . and keep on winning.

Keep Up to Date

Keep up with changes in the broad music world. How will synthesizers affect what you do? Computers? Electronics? You can't hide your head and hope that new trends and technologies will go away. They simply won't.

Do you like music video? Hate it? It doesn't really matter how you feel about it because it's here and will remain part of the music world. We all have to learn how to cope with what's happening.

We can reduce the stress caused by rapid change by trying not to judge until we understand. Remember all those musicians who said rock music wouldn't last? And remember all those rock musicians who said their music would obliterate everything else?

New markets appear, new technologies develop, new kinds of music are created, or old ones are resurrected. If you keep up, you'll be happier and more successful. If you rigidly refuse to watch what's happening, you'll be frustrated—and left behind.

One way to stay in tune is by reading in your field. Appendix A lists many excellent magazines that cover specific areas of music, and you will profit from reading them. You won't find most of these magazines at newsstands; you'll probably need to subscribe, but the cost of professional magazines and journals is tax deductible.

SOME IDEAS ABOUT MONEY

It's hard to be happy, or feel successful, when you're worried about the rent. Freelance musicians, with no steady work and with erratic income, are good prospects for money-caused ulcers. Here are a few ways to counter this ever-present problem.

Save money. Saving money may not be easy to do, but nothing is more important for your peace of mind. Figure out some way to put money aside. Ask your banker for help. To start, save any unexpected income; don't spend that $85 from the last-minute job you played Friday night. Since you weren't counting on it, save it.

You'll be able to relax when you have a growing savings plan, and you'll then be able to borrow more readily if you have to.

Every freelancer needs a cushion, a safety net. You'll have to provide your own, and saving is the best way to start.

Get health insurance. Buy hospital medical insurance through a group such as your union if you can. Anybody, even a musician, can have appendicitis or break an arm. With medical expenses as high as they are, a small accident or injury could be a financial disaster. Plan for the unexpected. Insurance isn't cheap, but it's far better than borrowing money to pay a hospital bill.

Set up an IRA. Try to establish an Individual Retirement Account or some other kind of long-term savings plan. This is really planning for the future—for the day when either you are physically unable to continue a full-time schedule of playing music or you choose active retirement. You'll also gain a sense of accomplishment and direction if you know you are getting ahead financially.

Know when to stop buying equipment. Don't spend all your money on musical equipment. Face it, there will *always* be something you *absolutely* need, but you'd have to be rich to keep up with the glittering inventory of a music store. Don't let the marketing wizards manipulate you into unmanageable debt. The latest synthesizer won't necessarily help your playing, nor will a new mouthpiece give you the ultimately perfect sound.

Resist the temptation to be a world-class consumer.

DON'T STOP

As your career grows, you'll probably find that you are increasingly in demand. People will know you, and you won't have to work as hard to find jobs. Don't stop now. You can't quit marketing your talents.

Keep adding to your PMMS as you acquire new skills and discover job possibilities. Continue to call on new clients and reinforce your relationship with old ones.

Remember; *if you're coasting, you're going downhill.* When you become successful, someone will always be poised to take your place.

ONE MORE TIME

The productive freelance music life can be wonderful. You can do what you enjoy—and get paid for it.

You can work in a variety of situations, each with new challenges and opportunities for success. You won't be limited by bureaucratic rules. You can get to know many interesting people and become well known in your community. You might even make more money from your enjoyable work than you ever considered possible.

You can succeed in the freelance music business if you work hard and don't stop. To an extent exciting to think about, you'll be in control of your own future.

I hope that the marketing methods described here will work as well for you as they have for me. If you use them, I'm sure you'll succeed.

Good luck!

Appendix A

A Sampling of Useful Publications

Keeping up with your area of music will be a lot easier if you stay in touch through magazines and journals. Here are some good ones; you'll find many others listed in the magazine directories in your library.

The American Harp Journal, 6331 Quebec Dr., Los Angeles, CA 90068. Covers activities of the American Harp Society.

American Music Teacher, 2113 Carew Tower, Cincinnati, OH 45202. Useful information for music teachers.

The American Organist, 815 2nd Ave., Suite 318, New York, NY 10017. Official journal of the American Guild of Organists.

Banjo Newsletter, Box 364, Greensboro, MD 21639. For banjo players.

Bluegrass Unlimited, Box 111, Broadrun, VA 22014. Emphasizes bluegrass and old-time country music.

Chamber Music America, 215 Park Ave. S., New York, NY 10003. Covers the field of chamber music.

Church Music Today, Box 369, Litchfield, CT 06759. For church organists and directors.

The Church Musician, 127 9th Ave., Nashville, TN 37234. For church musicians.

The Clarinet Magazine, University of Denver, CO 80210. Focuses on items of interest to clarinet players.

Clavier, 1418 Lake St., Evanston, IL 60204. For keyboard teachers and performers; emphasizes classical piano and pedagogy.

Contemporary Christian Music, P.O. Box 6300, Laguna Hills, CA 92653. Covers artistic, technical, and business aspects of contemporary gospel music.

The Diapason, 380 Northwest Highway, Des Plaines, IL 60016. Covers organ, harpsichord, carillon, and church music.

Downbeat, 222 W. Adams St., Chicago, IL 60606. Covers jazz and contemporary music.

Flute Talk, 200 Northfield Rd., Northfield, IL 60093. For all flute players.

Frets Magazine, GPI Publications, 20605 Lazaneo, Cupertino, CA 95014. For acoustic string players.

Guitar Player Magazine, GPI Publications, 20605 Lazaneo, Cupertino, CA 95014. For all guitarists.

Guitar World, 1115 Broadway, New York, NY 10010. Covers items of interest to guitarists, emphasis on pop music.

Instrumentalist, 200 Northfield Rd., Northfield, IL 60093. For band directors, teachers of instrumental music.

International Musician, 1500 Broadway, New York, NY 10036. Published by the American Federation of Musicians; sent to all members. Covers union and general professional news.

Jazz Educators Journal, Box 724, Manhattan, KS 66502. For band directors, music teachers interested in jazz instruction.

Jazz Times, 8055 13th St., Silver Spring, MD 20910. General-interest jazz magazine, emphasis on traditional jazz.

Jazziz, PO 8309, Gainesville, FL 32605. General-interest jazz magazine, emphasis on current players, performances, equipment.

Journal of Church Music, 2900 Queen Ln., Philadelphia, PA 19129. Newsletter for church musicians.

Keyboard Classics, 223 Katonah Ave., Katonah, NY 10536. Prints music for piano, organ in several graded editions.

Keyboard Magazine, GPI Publications, 20605 Lazaneo, Cupertino, CA 95014. For all keyboard players. Emphasis is on contemporary equipment and styles for classical and pop.

Modern Drummer, 1000 Clifton Ave., Clifton, NJ 07013. For all percussionists.

Modern Recording and Music, 1120 Old Country Rd., Plainview, NY 11803. Covers recording techniques.

Music and Sound Output, 220 Westbury Ave., Carle Place, NY 11514. Covers music business for musicians and sound people.

Music Educators Journal, 1902 Association Dr., Reston, VA 22091. For students and professionals in music education.

Music Magazine, Suite 202, 56 The Esplanade, Toronto, Ontario, Canada M5E, 1A7. Emphasizes classical music.

The Music Trades, PO 432, Englewood, NJ 07631. For music retailers, information about selling, equipment, industry developments.

MusicLine, Suite 201, 25231 Paseo De Alicia, Laguna Hills, CA 92653. General coverage of the gospel-music community.

Notes, 120 Claremont Ave., New York, NY 10027. Publication of the Music Library Association. Scholarly articles and reviews.

Ovation, 320 W. 57th St., New York, NY 10019. Covers classical music and recording/reproduction equipment.

Polyphony Magazine, Box 20305, Oklahoma City, OK 73156. Covers playing and recording electronic music.

The Singing News, PO Box 18010, Pensacola, FL 32523. Covers the gospel music community.

Songwriter Connection, Suite 106, 6640 Sunset Blvd., Hollywood, CA 90028. Inspiration and help for songwriters.

Suzuki World, 79 E. State St., Athens, OH 45701. For music teachers who are interested in the Suzuki method of instruction.

Symphony, PO Box 669, Vienna, VA 22180. Of interest to the symphony community.

Windplayer, PO 234, Northridge, CA 91328. For all brass and woodwind players; profiles and how-to information.

Appendix B
A Few Helpful Books

Your library or local bookstore has excellent books on financial management, sales techniques, tax planning, and, of course, music. These are only a sample of the many helpful resources you'll find.

The Art of Accompanying and Coaching by Kurt Adler. Da Capo Press, 1976.

Billboard Annual International Buyer's Guide. Billboard Publications, annual.

Business Letter Writing Made Simple by Irving Rosenthal and Harry Rudman. Doubleday, 1968.

Complete Book of Tax Deductions by Robert Holzman. Barnes and Noble, annual.

Getting Back to the Basics of Selling by Matthew J. Culligan. Ace Business Library, 1981.

The Grant Game by Lawrence Lee. Harbor Publishing, 1981.

How to Get Free Press by Toni Delacorte, Judy Kimsey, and Susan Halas. Harbor Publishing, 1981.

How to Master the Art of Selling by Tom Hopkins. Warner Books, 1982.

How to Sell Anything to Anybody by Joe Girard. Stanley H. Brown, 1979.

How to Set Up and Operate an Office at Home by Robert Scott. Scribner's, 1985.

How to Teach Piano Successfully by James Bastien. Kjos Publishing, 1977.

If They Ask You, You Can Write a Song by Al Kasha and Joel Hirschhorn. Simon and Schuster, 1979.

Making Money Making Music No Matter Where You Live by James W. Dearing. Writer's Digest Books, 1985.

The Memory Book by Harry Lorayne and Jerry Lucas. Ballantine, 1974.

Musical America Annual Directory. ABC Leisure Magazines, annual.

A Musician's Guide to the Road by Gary Burton. Billboard Books, 1981.

Need a Grant? The Individual's Guide to Grants. Judith B. Margolin. Plenum Press, 1983.

The New Financial Guide for the Self-Employed by John Ellis. Contemporary Books, 1981.

No Bull Selling by Hank Trishler. Bantam Books, 1985.

One Hundred and One Ways to Pay Less Taxes by the J.K. Lasser Tax Institute. Simon and Shuster, 1984.

Perfectly Legal by Barry Steiner and David Kennedy. John Wiley and Sons, annual.

Secrets of Closing the Sale by Zig Ziglar. Fleming H. Revell, 1984.

Smart Money Management by the J.K. Lasser Tax Institute. Simon and Schuster, 1985.

Songwriter's Market by Rand Ruggeberg, ed. Writer's Digest Books, annual.

Stop Forgetting by Dr. Bruno Furst. Doubleday, 1972.

Studio Recording for Musicians by Fred Miller. Amsco Publications, 1981.

This Business of Music by Sidney Shemel and M. William Krasilovsky. Billboard Publications, 1985.

The Unabashed Self-Promoter's Guide by Dr. Jeffrey Lant. JLA Publications, 1983.

Your Own Money by Sylvia Porter. Avon, 1983.

Appendix C

Music-Related Businesses

This is a small sampling of the thousands of businesses serving musicians. Their catalogs will serve as a basis for price and quality comparisons.

Ability Development, Box 887, Athens, OH 45701. Catalog of music learning aids, emphasis on Suzuki method, books, instruments.

Jamie Aebersold Records, 1211 Aebersold Dr., New Albany, IN 47150. Catalog of play-along records, especially jazz related.

Alkahest Agency, PO 12403, Atlanta, GA 30355. Booking agency specializing in college concerts.

Tino Anthony's Music Catalogue, 4001 East Fanfol, Phoenix, AZ 85028. How-to-play books.

Sam Ash Music Stores, 124 Fulton Ave., Hempstead, NY 11550. Telephone: 800-645-3518. Large discount music store, good for price comparison.

Ray Bloch Productions, 1500 Broadway, New York, NY 10036. National booking agency and convention-service company.

Charles Colin Universal Catalog, 315 W. 53rd St., New York, NY 10019. Catalog of how-to books and charts for musicians.

Day-Timers, Inc., PO 2368, Allentown, PA 18001. Variety of datebooks combined with effective time-management ideas.

Dexter Press, Route 303, West Nyack, NY 10994. Large color printing company. Can print color postcards, slick flyers, brochures.

Dover Publications, 31 East 2nd St., Mineola, NY 11501. Catalog of hard-to-find books, including copyright-free music illustrations.

Drum Drops, PO 3000, Woodland Hills, CA 91365. Recorded drum tracks for play-along use.

Eva-Tone Soundsheets, Inc., 4801 Ulmerton Rd., Clearwater, FL 33520. Produces flexible plastic records.

Everything's Music, 1155 Belvedere Rd., West Palm Beach, FL 33405. Catalog of music-related items.

Friendship House, 15624 Detroit Ave., Cleveland, OH 44107. Catalog of music-related items.

Hansen House/Maestro Library, 1870 West Ave., Miami Beach, FL 33139. Catalog of hard-to-find music books.

Lee-Myles Associates, Inc., 160 E. 56th St., New York, NY 10022. Designs and produces record covers.

Letraset USA, Inc., 40 Eisenhower Dr., Paramus, NJ 07652. Catalog of press-on letters and graphic aids. Available at local art dealers, or write for catalog and nearest dealer's name.

Mail-A-Music, PO 398148, Miami Beach, FL 33139. Publishes mail-order catalog of music and music-related books.

Mail Box Music, PO 341, Rye, NY 10580. Catalog of music books.

Mass Photo Co., 1439 Mayson St., Atlanta, GA 30324 or 1315 Waugh St., Houston, TX 77019. Produces publicity photos from your original.

Jack Morton Productions, 830 3rd Ave., New York, NY 10022. National booking agency, audiovisual producer, convention-service company.

The Music Bookshelf, PO 187, Fraser, MI 48026. Mail-order catalog of music books, particularly current interest.

Music Gifts, Box 351, Evanston, IL 60204. Catalog of music-related items.

Music Minus One, 43 W. 61st St., New York, NY 10023. Play-along records, large catalog.

National Repro Service, PO Box 56, Pickerel, WI 54465. Photo reproduction, posters, labels, cards, even personalized guitar picks.

Nebs Computer Forms, 12 South St., Townsend, MA 01469. All kinds of supplies for the computerized musician.

Appendix D
Selected Music Organizations

There are hundreds of organizations for musicians, from groups promoting a particular instrument to national labor unions. You can find other listings in the *Encyclopedia of Associations.*

Many of these organizations publish newsletters or magazines, handbooks or membership lists. Write for details on this excellent way to keep up with changes in your area of music. If addresses change, current listings can be found in the *Encyclopedia of Associations* in your library.

Accordion Federation of North America, 11438 Elmcrest St., El Monte, CA 91732.

American Bandmaster's Association, 2019 Bradford Dr., Arlington, TX 76010.

American Choral Director's Association, PO 6310, Lawton, OK 73506.

American Federation of Musicians, 1500 Broadway, New York, NY 10036.

American Federation of Television & Radio Artists (AFTRA), 1350 Avenue of the Americas, New York, NY 10019.

American Guild of Musical Artists, 1841 Broadway, New York, NY 10023.

American Guild of Organists, 815 Second Ave., New York, NY 10017.

American Guild of Variety Artists (AGVA), 1540 Broadway, New York, NY 10036.

American Harp Society, 6331 Quebec Dr., Los Angeles, CA 90068.

Big Band Academy of America, 1680 Vine St., Suite 1206, Hollywood, CA 90028.

Black Music Association, 1500 Locust, Suite 1905, Philadelphia, PA 19102.

Chamber Music America, 215 Park Ave. S., New York, NY 10003.

Country Music Foundation, 4 Music Square E., Nashville, TN 37203.

Fretted Instrument Guild of America, 2344 Oakley Ave., Chicago, IL 60608.

Gospel Music Association, 38 Music Square W., Nashville, TN 37202.

Guitar Foundation of America, Box 5311, Garden Grove, CA 90645.

Interlochen Center for the Arts, Interlochen, MI 49643.

International Clarinet Society, 7402 Wells Blvd., Hyattsville, MD 20783.

International Double Reed Society, 626 Lakeshore Dr., Monroe, LA 71203.

International Piano Guild, PO 1807, Austin, TX 78767.

International Polka Association, 4145 S. Kedzie Ave., Chicago, IL 60632.

International Rock 'n' Roll Music Association, PO 50111, Nashville, TN 37205.

International Society of Bassists, School of Music, Northwestern University, Evanston, IL 60201.

International Trombone Association, Music Dept., North Texas State University, Denton, TX 76203.

International Trumpet Guild, School of Music, Western Michigan University, Kalamazoo, MI 49008.

Louis Braille Foundation for Blind Musicians, 215 Park Ave. S., New York, NY 10003.

Music Teachers National Association, Inc., 2113 Carew Tower, Cincinnati, OH 45202.

Musicians' Foundation, 200 W. 55th St., New York, NY 10019.

Musicians' National Hot-Line Association, 277 E. 6100 S, Salt Lake City, UT 84107.

Nashville Songwriter's Association, 803 18th Ave. S., Nashville, TN 37203.

National Academy of Recording Arts and Sciences (NARAS), 4444 Riverside Dr., Suite 202, Burbank, CA 91505.

National Academy of Songwriters, 6772 Hollywood Blvd., Hollywood, CA 90028.

National Association for Music Therapy, 1133 15th St., NW, Washington, DC 20005.

National Association of Jazz Educators, PO Box 724, Manhattan, KS 66502.

The National Association of Pastoral Musicians, 1029 Vermont Ave., Washington, DC 20005.

National Band Association, PO 121292, Nashville, TN 37212.

National Federation of Music Clubs, 1336 N. Delaware St., Indianapolis, IN 46202.

National Flute Association, 805 Laguna, Denton, TX 76201.

National Old-Time Fiddler's Association, PO 636, Williamsburg, NM 87942.

Pedal Steel Guitar Association, PO 248, Floral Park, NY 11001.

Percussive Arts Society, 214 W. Main St., Urbana, IL 61801.

Phi Mu Alpha Sinfonia Fraternity, 10600 Old State Rd., Evansville, IN 47711.

Pianists Foundation of America, 210 5th Ave., New York, NY 10010.

Piano Technicians Guild, Inc., 1123 Dexter N., Seattle, WA 98109.

Society for the Preservation & Encouragement of Barber Shop Quartet Singing in America, 6315 Third Ave., Kenosha, WS 53140.

Society of the Classic Guitar, PO 566, New York, NY 10021.

Songsmith Society, PO 2601, Northbrook, IL 60062.

United States Information Agency, ICS/DA, Washington, DC 20547.

Universal Jazz Coalition, Inc., 156 Fifth Ave., Room 817, New York, NY 10010.

Violin Society of America, 85-07, Abington Rd., Kew Garden, NY 11415.

Appendix E
Special Events and Holidays

By checking into the reference books below—your library should have them—you'll be able to come up with a special event for each day of the year, something worth celebrating with music. There are, as *Chase's Annual Events* notes, presidential proclamations, national days, state days, sponsored events, astronomical phenomena, historical anniversaries, birthdays, and events from folklore.

What nightclub owner, apartment-complex manager, or country club social director could resist the lure of a party to celebrate the Kentucky Derby (early May), Thailand's Elephant Round-Up (mid-November), or the South Carolina Governor's Frog Jump and Egg Striking contest (early April)? If you want an excuse for suggesting a party, these books will give you plenty of official reasons for any day, and many weeks, of the year.

The American Book of Days by Jane M. Hatch. H.W. Wilson Co., 1977. Exhaustive list of birthdays, official holidays and other celebrated events.

Anniversaries and Holidays by Ruth W. Gregory. American Library Association, 1975. Excellent list of fixed and movable celebrations for both Western and Eastern countries.

Chase's Annual Events by W.D. and Helen Chase. Contemporary Books, 1985. Annual listing of 4,500 events of every sort. At least seven entries per day.

Festivals Sourcebook ed. Paul Wassermann. Gale Research, Detroit, 1977. Descriptions of thousands of fairs, festivals and community celebrations listed by subject of the event (ethnic, history, for example). A very useful book.

Here is a sampling of important—and frivolous—days to cele-

brate. The dates given are for 1985. Since most of these events are celebrated on different dates each year, be sure to consult the most current
reference book before you plan.

January

1 New Year's Day
3 Alaska admitted to the Union
4 Sherlock Holmes's birthday
6-13 National Bowling Week
8 Battle of New Orleans
8 Elvis Presley's birthday
11 Banana Boat Day (celebrates invention of disposable dish
     that holds banana splits)
13-19 Man Watchers' Week
15 Birthday of Martin Luther King, Jr.
16 Prohibition amendment repeal anniversary
18 Hat Day
19 Robert E. Lee's birthday
21 National Clean-Off-Your-Desk Day
24 California gold discovery anniversary
26 Rattlesnake Roundup (Whigham, GA)
27 Mozart's birthday

February

1-28 American Music Month
2 Groundhog Day
3 Bean-throwing festival (Japanese tradition)
3 Halfway point of winter
3-10 National New Idea Week
5 Weatherman's Day
10 World Marriage Day
14 Valentine's Day
16-19 Carnival (Brazil)
18 Bun Day (Ireland)
18 George Washington's birthday
19 Mardi Gras
23-March 2 Chinese New Year celebration
23 George Frederick Handel's birthday

March

    1 National Pig Day
    2 Texas Independence Day
 4-10 National Procrastination Week
14-17 Saint Patrick's Day
   15 Buzzard's Day (Hinckley, OH)
   15 Ides of March
   18 Rudolph Diesel's birthday
   20 Earth Day
   21 First day of spring
   21 Johann Sebastian Bach's birthday
   22 National Goof-off Day
24-31 King Neptune Frolic Week (Sarasota, FL)
   25 Greek Independence Day
31-April 6 Holy Week

April

    1 April Fool's Day
 1-30 Cherry blossom festivals around country
    5 Governor's Frog Jump and Egg Striking Contest (Springfield, SC)
    7 Easter Sunday (date varies between March 22 and April 25)
 7-13 Harmony Week (barbershop quartet singing)
   12 Anniversary of the Big Wind (Mt. Washington, NH, Celebrates highest recorded wind velocity, 231 mph)
14-20 Lefty Awareness Week
   15 Income taxes due
   15 National Griper's Day
   18 Zimbabwe Independence Day
21-27 Professional Secretaries' Week
   23 Shakespeare's birthday
   24 Running of the Rodents (Louisville, KY)
   27 World Cow Chip Throwing Championship (Beaver, OK)

May

 1-31 Correct Posture Month
    1 Law Day

1 May Day
3 International Tuba Day
4 Kentucky Derby
4 One Hundred Tons of Fun Day (celebrates large people)
5-12 National Music Week
10 Golden Spike Day (Promontory Point, UT)
10-12 National Strange Music Weekend (Olive Hill, KY)
12 Mother's Day
16-25 International Pickle Week
17-19 Fertility Rites Celebration (the Philippines)
18 Mount St. Helen's eruption anniversary
20 Victoria Day (Canada)
24-June 9 Spoleto Festival (Charleston, SC)
25 African Freedom Day
26 John Wayne's birthday
27 Memorial Day

June

4 Old Maids' Day
8 Queen's official birthday (England)
10 Judy Garland's birthday
14 Flag Day
15 Smile Power Day
16 Father's Day
19 Garfield's birthday (the cat)
21 Summer begins
22 National Fink Day
27-29 Watermelon Thump (Luling, TX)

July

1 Canada Day
1 Caribbean Day
1-31 National Baked Bean Month, Ice Cream Month, Hot Dog Month
3-August 15 Dog Days (hottest of year)
4 Louis Armstrong's birthday
4 Independence Day
7-13 "Be Nice to New Jersey" Week
11 National Cheer Up the Lonely Day
22 Pied Piper of Hamelin anniversary

August

1-7 National Clown Week
1 Switzerland National Day
3 Twins' Day
8-11 National Polka Festival (Hunter, NY)
11 Family Day
15 National Failures' Day
15 National Relaxation Day
17 David Crockett's birthday
19 National Aviation Day
23 Great American Duck Race (Deming, NM)
23-25 Old Time Fiddlers' Contest (Carson City, NV)
26 Women's Equality Day
31 International Zucchini Festival

September

2 Labor Day
4 City of Los Angeles birthday
5 "Be Late for Something" Day
7 Buddy Holly's birthday
8 Grandparents' Day
12-21 "Snack-A-Pickle" time
13 "Blame Someone Else" Day
15-21 National Singles Week
16-17 Rosh Hashanah
22 Autumn begins
26 George Gershwin's birthday
28-29 International Whistle-Off contest (Carson City, NV)

October

1-31 Oktoberfest celebrations all around the United States
3-12 National Pasta week
9 John Lennon's birthday
12 Columbus Day
15 National Grouch Day
16 National Boss's Day
28 Statue of Liberty birthday
29 Stock market collapse anniversary
31 Halloween

November

1 All Saints' Day
2 Sadie Hawkins Day
3 Sandwich Day
6 John Philip Sousa's birthday
9 Great Northeast Power Blackout anniversary (1965)
11 Veterans' Day
18 Mickey Mouse's birthday
21 World Hello Day
24-25 "D.B. Cooper" hijack anniversary
24 Scott Joplin's birthday
28 Thanksgiving Day

December

1-25 Celebrations, festivals, tours of homes, concerts for Christmas season throughout United States
1 Pasadena Doo-Dah Parade
8-15 Hanukkah
12 Frank Sinatra's birthday
14 Discovery of the South Pole anniversary
16 Beethoven's birthday
16 Boston Tea Party anniversary
20 Underdog Day
21 Winter begins
25 Christmas Day
31 New Year's Eve

Appendix F

Resume

JIM GIBSON AND HIS BAND PROVIDE MUSIC FOR MANY
COMPANY, SOCIAL AND ASSOCIATION FUNCTIONS

Atlanta's Jim Gibson, as a single pianist and with bands ranging from three to twelve pieces, has played for hundreds of top companies and associations across the South. Jim's bands have performed for banquets, dances, shows, award presentations, grand opening ceremonies, ground-breakings, weddings, promotion and retirement parties and many other kinds of special events.

His music has been enjoyed from The Homestead (Virginia) to New Orleans, and from Miami to Hilton Head Island. He has also worked extensively in Europe, primarily in Paris, and in Florence, Italy.

The musicians in Jim's bands, all well-schooled and experienced, pride themselves on their professionalism and versatility, and can provide a variety of music from country to classical, and from polkas to pop.

Jim's experience has clearly shown that most company, social and association groups are composed of people of different ages and backgrounds, and his success in this competitive field comes from his ability to provide just the kind of music the occasion requires.

His own background has prepared him well for this kind of varied musical work. He comes from a musical family; Jim's mother is a piano teacher, and his sister is a concert pianist and teacher. His academic training (M.A., English) and work experiences (teaching, public relations, writing), have given him the musical and personal background to be at home in any situation, and his music reflects this wide-ranging experience.

Here is a partial list of companies and associations that Jim and his bands have served from 1978 through early 1983.

(<u>Boldface</u> indicates repeat engagements.)

A T & T
Aaron Rents
AEA Services
Abbott Laboratories
Academy of General Dentistry
Academy of Psychological Medicine
Ackerman and Company
Adolfo Porrato Doria
Allis-Chalmers
American Apparel Manufacturer's Ass'n
American Bar Ass'n
American Electroplater's Society
American Family Life
American Logistics Ass'n
American Right of Way Ass'n
American Society of Landscape Architects
American Society of Nondestructive Testing
American Water Works Ass'n
Amoco Chemicals Corp
Armstrong-Blum Co
Arthur Anderson & Co.
Association of Surgical Technologists
Atlanta Athletic Club

Atlanta Flames Fan Club
Atlanta Postal Supervisors
Atlanta Ski Club
Atlanta Urologic Society
Atlanta Wire Works
Avon
BFA Educational Media
Borden, Inc
Brooks Shoes
Bud Antle Company
Buick
Builder Marts of America
Business Week Magazine
CBS-TV
CPA Associates
Cadillac
Cambridge Plan International
Canvas Products Ass'n
Caswell Realty Co
Champion Home Builders
Cheesebrough-Ponds
Chemical Bank of New York
Chem-Nut

193

Chevrolet
Circle Steel Co
Cobb County Dental Society
Coca-Cola USA
Combined Insurance
Commerical Union Insurance
Commissioned Officers Ass'n,
   U.S. Public Health Service
Cooper Group
Coronado Paint Co
Corrugated Converters
Davies-Young Co
Delta Airlines
Distron
Driver-Harris Co
Dun's Marketing Service
Dynamic Metals, Inc
Eastman Kodak
Eaton Corporation
The Economy Company
Ewing Brothers
Exchange Natiional Bank
FTD Directors
Family Weekly Magazine
Federal Express
Finance America
First Alabama Bank
First Federal Savings and
   Loan of Atlanta
Food Manufacturing Sales
   Executives
Foote and Davies
Ford Motor Co
Frosty Acres Brands
Fuji Photo Film
General Electric
General Electric Credit
General Electric Credit
   Union of Rome, GA
Georgia Beer Wholesaler's
   Ass' Ass'n
Georgia Chamber of
   Commerce
Georgia Dental Ass'n
Georgia Distilled Spirits
   Institute
Georgia Farm Bureau
Georgia Federation of
   Democratic Women
Georgia Florists' Ass'n
Georgia Mining Ass'n
Georgia Miss Teenager
   Pagent
Georgia-Pacific
Georgia Psychiatric Ass'n

Georgia Savings and Loan
   League
Georgia Telephone Ass'n
Gerber Products
W. R. Grace & Co
Grand Trunk Corporation
Graphic Associates
Gulfstream Aviation
Harper & Row
Haskins and Sells
HealthCo
Hercules, Inc
Hub Floral Corp
Hyatt Hotels, International
   Sales
I. B. M.
Industrial Fabrics Ass'n
   International
International Systems
J. C. Penney Bridal Fair
Jewish National Fund
Johns Manville
Josten's Rings
Junior League of Atlanta
Kemper Insurance
LaChoy Food Products
Lederle Laboratories
Liberty Life Insurance
Life of Georgia
Life Office Management
   Ass'n
Lombardini
The Loveable Co
McDonough Construction Co
Marble Institute of America
Market Forge
Mayfield Carpets
Medical Society of Virginia
Meldisco Shoe Corp
Mellon Bank
Mental Health Nursing
   Symposium
Mercury Marine
The Midnight Sun
Milton Bradley
Morley Incentives
Natn'l Ass'n of Industrial
   and Office Parks
Natn'l Automatic Laundry
   and Cleaning Ass'n
Natn'l Chemical Credit Ass'n
Natn'l Fertilizer Solutions
   Ass'n
Natn'l Governor's Ass'n
Natn'l Railroad Construction
   and Maintenance Ass'n

Natn'l Transportation Union
Natn'l Utility Contractors
   Ass'n
Natn'l Wheel and Rim Ass'n
Nestle
Newsweek Magazine
Northern Telecom
Peachtree World of Tennis
Peat, Marwick and Mitchell
Phoenix Debs Socitey
Piedmont Development Co.
Planning Executives Institute
Pontiac
Pratt and Whitney
Printing Ass'n of Georgia
Professional Picture Framers
   of America
Radio Shack
RC Cola
Richey TV
Rich's
Rock Tenn Packaging Co
Saks Fifth Avenue
Scientific Atlanta
Service Masters Industries
Southern Company
Southern Bell
Southern Decorating Products
   Ass'n
Southern Federal Tax
   Institute
Southern Jewelry
   Travellers
Southern Seedsmen's Ass'n.
Spring Manufacturers'
   Institute
State Farm Insurance
Sun Life Insurance
3M Company
Toyota
Troutman, Sanders, Lockerman
   and Ashmore
Uniroyal
University of Georgia Law
   Alumni
University of Miami Alumni
   Ass'n
Volkswagen of America
Water Pollution Control
   Federation
Westinghouse
Weather Channel
Winthrop Laboratories
F. W. Woolworth
World Service Insurance
Writing Instrument Mfrs' Ass'n
   ....and many more

Index

Other Books to Help You Make Money and the Most of Your Music Talent

Songwriter's Market—The only annual directory that gives detailed information on where and how to market your songs. Includes more than 2,000 listings of song buyers, with details on who to contact, how to submit your songs, royalty rates, and how to get your songs heard by the right people. Plus: articles and interviews with music industry experts. 432 pages/$15.95

The Craft of Lyric Writing, by Sheila Davis—Davis, a successful lyricist, composer, and teacher, analyzes more than 30 successful lyrics to show you why they caught the music industry's attention. You'll learn how to select the most effective song form for your lyrics; handle rhyme, meter, and beat; edit and rewrite for top results; and choose titles that will help your songs sell. 350 pages/$17.95

Making Money Making Music (No Matter Where You Live), by James Dearing—Dearing shows you how to build a solid financial base with your group or band (with solid advice on getting and keeping your group together) as the first step in developing a profitable music career. You'll also learn how to diversify your talent to expand your income—and even find proven methods for getting a record contract. 320 pages/$12.95, paperback

The Performing Artist's Handbook, by Janice Papolos—Here are the business basics you need if you're an instrumentalist or vocalist seeking to advance your career in major symphony orchestras, opera companies, chamber ensembles, and on concert stages. Papolos fully covers all the steps vital to your success, including self-promotion, resumes, business letters, debut recitals, and much more. 219 pages/$15.95

Use this coupon to order your copies!
